FAMILY
AFFAIRS

FAMILY AFFAIRS

•

Jillian Dagg

AVALON BOOKS
NEW YORK

Published by Thomas Bouregy & Co., Inc.
401 Lafayette Street, New York, NY 10003

PRINTED IN THE UNITED STATES OF AMERICA
ON ACID-FREE PAPER
BY HADDON CRAFTSMEN, BLOOMSBURG, PENNSYLVANIA

For Lou, Jo-Anne, Gayle, and Dan

Chapter One

Kim's office phone buzzed and the light began to flash. A little annoyed by the interruption, she quickly saved her current document with the mouse, then reached past her computer for the receiver. Brushing aside a strand of gleaming copper hair, she answered abruptly, "Kim Russell, Assistant Art Director."

"Kim. It's Josie."

"Hey. It's good to hear from you," Kim told her younger sister. "What's going on in Valleyview?" Not that Kim was involved in life in the small Kentucky town anymore. She made her life in Chicago now. She stared at her monitor. The ideas for the perfume advertisement had a five o'clock deadline.

"Valleyview is still the same. But I'm not the same. I'm on top of the world. I'm getting married, Kim."

Pressing deadlines forgotten for a moment, Kim whooped, "Great news. When? Who? I didn't know you were dating anyone. You never said when you visited me here in January."

"I wasn't sure then. We had only been out on a few dates. Now it's serious. I'm going to marry Brand Stanton."

Kim's stomach sank so low she felt weak, and the busy office beyond her own work station spun before her eyes. The Stanton family was the cream of Valleyview society. The Stanton boys had been driven to private schools in chauffeured cars, while the rest of them caught the lumbering school buses to the local school. The Stantons went to Harvard. Moira Russell, Kim's mother, had been their housekeeper and Kim used to help her.

Kim couldn't believe she had heard the news right. She finally said, "You're actually going to marry a Stanton?"

"Yes. Aren't I going up in the world?"

"You sure are. From housekeeper's daughter to bride."

Josie made a sound that wasn't quite a laugh. "What difference does that make, Kim? Mom hasn't worked for them since I was about twelve years old. Anyone would think it mattered."

Kim heard the frustration in Josie's voice. "Why? What's happened?"

"Well, Dad's okay with it. But Mom's being difficult. She thinks I should reconsider."

Kim's mouth felt as if it wouldn't work very well. She straightened the telephone cord and said, "Are you going to?"

"No way. It's all planned. We're getting married in three weeks, just before the Kentucky Derby, so lots of guests can attend both. The Stanton family is helping with the wedding. Dad can't afford a wedding for people of their stature, obviously, therefore we're keeping it simple and having the ceremony in our church and the reception in the gardens of Stanton Farm."

"And Dad doesn't mind the help?"

"No. He's had a good long chat with Frank and they decided to share the cost. It's fair these days, isn't it?"

Kim thought her father probably had felt humiliated, but he wouldn't let Josie know there was anything amiss. Kim wanted to cry. All she had done to rise above her background in Valleyview was now crumbling before her eyes. If Josie married a Stanton, Kim herself would be forced to socialize with the family she knew had treated her mother wrongly ten years ago. Her mother was probably thinking along the same lines. No wonder Moira wasn't happy with the plans.

"How did you get involved with him, Josie?"

"My boss, Tyler Matheson, is his lawyer, and one day Brand came in the office to have lunch with Tyler, but Tyler was stranded in a snowstorm in Ohio, so I went to lunch with Brand instead. We just hit it off. We knew right away, but we've waited a while to make it look not too whirlwind. Even so, Mom thinks I'm rushing things. And I'm not. I'm going through with it, Kim. I'm getting married. I don't care what you all say."

Kim leaned her elbow on the desk and rubbed her forehead in frustration. This didn't appear to be anything she could talk her sister out of. But then Josie wouldn't really understand why Kim and Mom were so upset. She hadn't been at Stanton Farm on the night Kim had heard Frank lash into her mother so cruelly. The exact words had been blurred, but Kim had heard the yelling voices that made her stomach collapse with fear. Then her mother had rushed from the sitting room. She was sobbing as she grabbed Kim's hand and hauled her to the front door. Brett Stanton, Brand's older brother, had seen them out the door. Usually he had a smile for Kim, even a teasing word or two. But not that night. She would never forget the look of disdain on Brett's handsome face as she hurried out the front door with her mother.

Her mother had started the family car and then drove fast out of the farm gates. Moira Russell had gunned the engine along the highway, and the car shot forward at great speed. Scared, Kim had hung onto the handhold. She had never seen her mother so furious, so upset. Moira was choking on her sobs.

Finally, as they reached the edge of Valleyview, Moira seemed to calm down. She slowed the car and said, "Not a word about this to anyone, Kim. Don't mention it to your father, your sister, or anyone. Forget it ever happened. Promise."

Kim had been shaking. "I promise. But what happened?"

"That's not important. I'm just not going to be working there anymore. Just forget everything."

But Kim had never forgotten anything, and she often wondered what the fight between Moira Russell and Frank Stanton had been about. She presumed Moira hadn't performed her duties as well as Frank would have liked, and Frank had fired her. Her mother always had a lot of pride.

She wouldn't want to admit that her housekeeping services had been lacking in any respect. Kim didn't think they were, although Moira had smoked at the time and Kim recalled that her mother once dropped ashes by mistake and burned a patch on one of the pieces of antique bedroom furniture. Moira had polished the dark scald as well as she could, then placed a white lace doily over the mark. Occasionally Kim would lift the mat and peer at the mark. She thought that was probably one of the reasons for the dismissal, even if she thought it was unfair.

"Are you still there Kim?" Josie asked.

Kim's usual control left her. Because of what had happened that night, she was distraught at the news of Josie's wedding. The event would cause a huge disruption in their family. It would change the entire landscape of their future. Her poor mother would have to face Frank Stanton year in and year out for the rest of her life. "Yes. I'm here. But why such short notice, Josie?" She hoped her sister wasn't in trouble and being forced to marry a Stanton.

"I know what you're thinking," Josie said with a chuckle. "But it's not that."

Kim sighed with relief. "Then why the rush?"

"Well, the 'boys'—that's what their parents call Brand and Brett—are taking over the farm now. Frank and Liz are retiring and going to live in Arizona as soon as they return from a world cruise. They're leaving soon, and we want to get married before they leave. Brand and I will have the guest apartment at Stanton Farm until our house is built on another part of the property. I'll show you the house that's being built when you're here."

"It sounds great, Josie." Kim didn't feel she could say anything else.

"You will come to the wedding and stand up for me, won't you?" Josie asked.

Kim hadn't given any thought to being one of the wedding party. "Yes. I could, I suppose."

"Sound cheerful about it, Kimmy."

Kim decided she had better buck herself up. After all, it would only be a wedding. When it was over she would return to Chicago. But not her mother. Moira would have to stay there. She must be facing a dilemma. She loved her younger daughter. She wouldn't want to jeopardize Josie's happiness. But, oh dear, it must be embarrassing for her. The future suddenly appeared difficult and complicated.

"Kim. What is the matter? If you're worried about how they think of us because mother was their housekeeper, then you don't have to. The fact hasn't been mentioned, and Brand doesn't care." Josie sighed dramatically. "And *I* don't care, Kim. You've always been so hung up about status. It doesn't matter. Love conquers all, you know."

"Maybe in books," Kim said wryly.

"Kim, you're so cynical. Wait until you fall in love."

Kim didn't have time for love. She had been too intent on making a living and elevating her advertising career. Her dates were casual, usually with a group of friends who felt the same way. Her roommate Hilary had gone home to New York for a while to visit her parents because there was an old boyfriend there, an old flame she hoped to rekindle. Kim didn't have anyone like that. Any boy she had dated had either left Valleyview or married.

"*Kim,* you keep going silent. I want you by my side at the wedding. You will come?"

Kim let out a little puff of breath. "Yes. Of course, Josie. I'll arrange some vacation."

"Can you come home a week ahead of time so you can fit your dress?"

"I'll try. I'll call you back from home tonight, when I've told my boss."

"That will be great. By the way, Brett is standing up for Brand, so he'll be your partner."

That news didn't sit well with Kim either. She

had hoped never to see Brett again after that night. She said hurriedly, "I thought Brett would be married."

"No way. I told you, he's been busy taking over the horse breeding business from his dad. He hasn't got a girlfriend either, so you're in luck."

Luck! "I don't care a hoot about Brett Stanton, Josie."

Josie laughed. "You might when you see him. He's really good-looking. And he is a bit like you. He's very tenacious about things. You know, how you don't let go very easily? Like for instance, you have to forget Mom was their housekeeper. It's nothing to do with my wedding."

Kim wasn't particularly comfortable with this description of herself, but she feigned a light laugh, and said, "Okay. I'll behave." She saw her boss peer out of her office window at her. "I have to go, Josie. My boss is wandering around. I'll talk to you later."

"Okay. Thanks, Kim. I'm looking forward to seeing you. I love you. And I miss you."

"I miss you and I love you too, Josie," Kim said sincerely before she hung up the phone. Then she buried her face in her hands. She had never mentioned that evening again to her mother. Now she wondered if, like herself, her mother was reliving it? And what about Frank Stanton? Had he forgotten? And Brett? He had been there. He knew.

"Are you all right, Kim?"

Kim glanced up to look at her boss, Rosemary Tilbury, a tall, slim nervous woman in her late thirties. Lately Rosemary had begun to drive Kim a little crazy, although when Kim first came to Carlton and Clark Advertising, she had admired Rosemary no end. She had it all: a good-looking husband, a smart twelve-year-old son, and a beautiful home in the suburbs. Plus a super career with C&C. Now, in the lunchroom, she had heard rumors of a divorce, and it proved to Kim that a career, husband, and family didn't meld. It was a firm belief she held, and she intended to stick to it. All her friends who had married early were either divorced or having problems. Women she knew were juggling home and husband with their careers, and it was wearing them out. One by one the careers got shelved or expectations pared down. Kim didn't back down from her belief that she needed to stay single. Josie was right. She was stubborn, but it made her focused in her job.

Rosemary cleared her throat. "Kim?"

"Oh, I'm fine," Kim said, not mentioning her sister's call because the company frowned on personal phone calls. "I was just thinking about the ad I'm working on."

Rosemary came around to stand behind her. Kim hated people staring over her shoulder. She gently touched the mouse and her ad appeared. In the light of traumatic family affairs, the design seemed unappealing.

Rosemary leaned forward. "It looks good, Kim. Remember—we need it by five."

"I know. I'll have it ready before then."

"Good. Don't let me disturb you then."

Rosemary returned to her own office, and Kim began to move graphics around on the screen once more, deciding nothing could disturb her as much as the phone call from Josie. Nothing disturbed her like news from Valleyview.

Kim shouldered her carry-on and pushed her suitcase along the floor by the handle. Brett Stanton was picking her up at the airport. Kim had argued this decision with Josie when she called to tell her, but Josie had insisted the plans must stick. Brett was away on business and would drop by the airport on his return trip on Sunday. It seemed the Stanton family had everything worked out, and one of the arrangements was pairing the best man and the maid of honor. But she could have waited for their pairing to begin.

Therefore, why couldn't they have sent a chauffeur? That way she would have been able to sit in the back of a limousine and watch the green Kentucky landscape, giving her a chance to settle her nerves. Besides, it would have been interesting to drive into Valleyview in a limo. It might have given her some confidence, confidence she badly needed to make the trip home.

Kim walked to an area where she might see Brett, or vice versa, although she doubted he knew what she looked like now that she was older. And she wasn't sure she would recognize him either. She sat down on one of the seats and smoothed her black slacks and thigh-length jacket she wore with a white silk top. She crossed her legs and gazed at her black leather high-heeled shoes. She felt she was going to look far too "big city" for Valleyview. So what, she decided, tucking a wisp of hair back into the upswept style with just a hint of fashionable untidiness about it. She *was* big city now. That was what leaving Valleyview had been all about. And she should be feeling thrilled, because she had a fantastic promotion to consider.

After arranging her vacation, and in the midst of her rush to leave the office, John Clark had called her into his office yesterday afternoon to tell her Rosemary was leaving and to ask if Kim would be interested in the position. She was definitely interested. She had been working in the main office as an assistant for three years now, and a promotion would mean more responsibility and more money. Since Rosemary still had a month to go yet, John didn't expect her to make a snap decision. He'd handed her an envelope containing the details of the offer, to be perused at her leisure. Kim had been pleased they'd given her final decision a respite. She hadn't had a chance yet to look inside the envelope. It lay unopened in her suitcase, awaiting some quiet time. It certainly gave her something to keep her mind occupied, instead of focusing on what was to come in Valleyview.

Kim felt someone watching her and looked over to a man wearing black western boots, snug jeans, and a black leather jacket over a black and red crew-neck sweater. Brown hair, thick and straight, brushed his collar and framed, even from this distance, dark brows, a strong nose, sensual mouth, and a square, distinct jaw. Kim's pulse hummed. Part of her, although she was reluctant to admit it to her girlfriends in the city, was attracted to a rugged horseman—what she secretly considered a real man. When she was in the city with her friends she hid those feelings, denying they existed. She abhorred that part of her. It reminded her that beneath her veneer she was still the country girl she'd been raised as. She stared once more at her sophisticated shoes. She had risen above her lowly background. She had.

But she let her eyes linger on the man once more, and suddenly she saw recognition in his expression. She realized with a start he was Brett. He strode over to her.

"Hi. Kim?"

She rose to her feet, her hazel eyes meeting his brilliant green gaze. She smiled her office smile. "Brett. How are you?"

"Pleased you looked my way. I was wondering how I was going to find you. But the hair—I should have known." He put out his hand to her.

Kim ignored an impulse to touch her hair to confirm his comment, and they shook hands briefly but firmly. The attraction Kim had experienced from a distance pulsed through her body now he was up close. To be attracted to Brett was the last thing she needed in this difficult situation. She turned away to deal with her luggage.

But Brett intercepted, and Kim noticed the way his muscles rippled beneath his leather jacket as he picked up her two bags. He was tough and muscular from a life of manual work, for despite his wealth, Frank Stanton believed in giving his boys hands-on treatment with the horses they bred on the farm. There was also the regime of horse riding. Brett was an accomplished rider, as she was herself. That had come as part of living in Valleyview, even if the horses Brett rode were of better quality than the ones Kim had ridden at her uncle's riding school.

"Any more luggage?" he asked, glancing around.

"No. No more luggage."

"You travel light?"

"I'm only staying a week."

"That's all?" he said.

"Yes, that's all. It's all the vacation I could get at such short notice."

"I understand. However, most women I know travel with an entourage of luggage."

"Well, I'm not most women you know," she retorted, and then regretted the outburst. But she couldn't help it. Her stomach was tied up in knots inside. The emotion had to be released somehow.

One of his dark eyebrows rose. "What's your problem?"

She realized she shouldn't have let her tension show. She shook her head and shrugged her shoulders. "No problem."

He shifted the bags more comfortably in his hands. "In that case, let's get moving."

Carrying her bags Brett strode off, with Kim

walking fast beside him. They left the terminal and located his black four-wheel-drive utility vehicle. Once the luggage was stowed, they settled side by side in the front seats. Brett drove out of the airport and onto a highway ramp.

Once on the Interstate, Brett asked, "So how are you?"

"Oh, fine. A bit tired. I've had a busy morning traveling."

"True. But I've also been traveling. I flew into Lexington from New York this morning. It would have been easier if you'd flown into Lexington, not Louisville. Then I wouldn't have had this extra drive."

"Well, I didn't have a pick of flights. I didn't ask for you to come and fetch me, Brett."

"It's expected," he said. "So just cool it a bit."

They had gotten off to a bad start, Kim thought, looking out of the window, but all she saw were a few raindrops splattering against the glass, and she wished they didn't look like tears. Kim pressed the heel of her hand to her soon-to-be aching forehead. She had experienced constant pressure ever since Josie's phone call, and now she was on the brink of exploding.

"Are you feeling okay?" Brett asked.

No. She wasn't. She had been the Stanton housekeeper's daughter. The *disgraced* Stanton housekeeper's daughter. Now she was returning as the sister of a Stanton bride. Josie, why Brand of all the men in Valleyview? Kim hadn't spoken at length to her mother, but she was sure Moira was asking the same question. Her father, of course, didn't know about Moira's abrupt dismissal. He thought she had left the Stanton job at her own initiative because she was fed up with housecleaning and wanted to work somewhere else. So his only thoughts might be that at last he had access to the elite of Valleyview, instead of merely their horses.

They continued to speed east along I-64 and Kim decided it wouldn't take long to reach Valleyview at this rate. Everything was moving far too fast for Kim. Even though she'd had three weeks to prepare herself, she still wasn't ready to face the town and her family. Panic reached up and grasped her throat, and she touched Brett's arm with trembling fingers. The leather of his jacket was very supple, extremely expensive—the Stanton style. It made her recall how she used to covet his home when she accompanied her mother to do housekeeping chores. It also reminded her of the separate nature of their lives. His in the big farmhouse, son of the wealthy horse breeder. Hers down in the village, daughter of the blacksmith who served the wealthy horse men.

Even so, she clutched at him.

He looked at her with one eyebrow raised.

Kim cleared her throat. "Could we stop for a while? I would like some coffee."

"Don't you want to get home?"

He didn't know Valleyview wasn't really home to her anymore. She had exiled herself from her birthplace on purpose. Something he wouldn't understand because he was so well thought of. "Not quite yet. I need to stop, Brett. I have to collect my thoughts."

"Why, where are they?"

Kim heard real humor for the first time. "All over the place. You can stop anywhere. It doesn't have to be a fancy restaurant." Kim heard the desperation in her voice. She truly needed time to collect herself. "I need some space, Brett. Just a cooling down time."

"I would have thought the plane trip would have been enough."

"No. It wasn't."

"This is a wedding, not a funeral."

"Don't argue with me, Brett." Didn't he understand? Or maybe he didn't remember. She hoped he didn't remember. Maybe Frank Stanton dismissed all his housekeepers in the same ugly manner, and Brett didn't remember one from the other.

"I'm not arguing. I'll stop. I need a cup of coffee as well."

He slowed down and took the next exit. He parked outside a cozy-looking restaurant with a dark wooden exterior. Kim climbed from the vehicle, gratified to feel the moist spring air on her face. She gulped in a couple of breaths.

Brett touched her waist. "Are you sure you're okay?"

His fingers against her waist ignited her attraction once more, and Kim took a step forward to force his hand to drop. "Yes, I'm fine. I just needed to stop for a while." She knew she sounded brisk and ungrateful but she couldn't help it.

He moved up beside her. "Let's go get that coffee. Now you're starting to worry me."

"I'm all right." But she wasn't all right. She was a mess. And she was making a big mistake by letting him see the mess. She was already at a disadvantage with him on a social level. She should be acting cool and sophisticated, but she didn't feel cool and sophisticated. She felt confused and frightened about the situation she was going home to.

"You do look very pale." Brett's eyes moved

over her features. "Or maybe it's because your hair is so bright."

She touched her hair this time. "You keep mentioning my hair color."

"Well, it's a fascinating color. Not really red, not really blond."

"It's real."

"I know it is. Don't get so defensive. What's really wrong?"

"You wouldn't understand."

"You could try me."

"Oh no, Brett. Let's just get some coffee. I really do need some. I'm getting a headache."

He loosened his shoulders as if he needed to relax. "Okay. Come on."

Kim followed Brett into the warmth and coffee aroma of the restaurant. Right away she knew that this haven would provide her some solace, even with Brett as her companion. He led her to a comfortable table overlooking the parking lot. A waitress came over and put menus down in front of them.

"Just coffee?" he asked Kim.

"Yes, just coffee." Kim loosened the buttons of her jacket and smoothed the flat gold chain at her throat.

Brett seemed to drag his eyes from her before saying to the waitress, "Two coffees. That's all."

The waitress's smile was brighter for Brett, and Kim felt a stab of annoyance. Now that Brand had been snapped up by Josie, Brett was probably Valleyview's most eligible bachelor and had all the women after him.

The coffees were poured into thick white cups. Kim added cream. Brett's remained black.

"I'm surprised you never married," Brett stated.

Kim hid any surprise that he should be thinking similar thoughts to her own. However, she decided the comment was more in the line of making conversation than any desire to know more about her. She placed her spoon in the saucer. "Why would that be?"

He shrugged. "People get married."

"Some do, so I've heard."

He smiled. "But not you?"

"No. Not me. You're not married either, are you? I would have expected you to be carrying on the Stanton name by now."

"So does my father, but . . ." He rubbed his jaw rather endearingly. "I don't know, Kim. I just haven't met anyone who lights my fire. What's your excuse?"

"Career has been important to me," she admitted, wondering what type of woman it would take to light Brett's fire. Feeling breathless at the very thought of Brett being in love, she picked up her cup and sipped, savoring the taste. She changed the subject. "Nice coffee. Good roadside traveling fare. I'm so used to office gruel."

He kept his eyes on her. "What is your career?"

"Magazine advertising."

"Like it?"

"It complements my graphic arts training."

"Do you work on a computer?"

"Yes, I do. Why?"

"We've recently had a small office complex built at the farm and we're expanding our computer systems. We do quite a bit of advertising in magazines internationally. Usually, we have a graphics company handle the artwork, but I think we need someone to do it for us at the farm."

"I'm sure it would be a great job."

"Not for you?" he said.

"Are you offering me the job?"

He smiled. "Let's say I'm putting out some feelers. If not you, maybe one of your colleagues in Chicago. Someone who wants a quieter life."

"I could ask," she said. "I already have a good job. A good life. Lots of friends. I share a really nice apartment with a girlfriend."

Brett twisted his cup around in the saucer. "You don't miss the country?"

"No." She spoke quickly and knew as usual

she had fibbed. Deep down inside, where she didn't dare go too often, was the life she had left behind. Sometimes she would look out of her office window and watch the bustle of the traffic and see before her eyes rolling green fields and horses, and she felt a deep pang of nostalgia. Sometimes when she was walking around the crowded city, she didn't want to be there. But she kept all that emotion to herself, because it went away most of the time and wasn't always part of her.

"You're lucky. I couldn't stomach living in a city, but then that's me. I like wide open spaces."

"That's you," she said coolly. "I'm me. We're different." We always have been, she thought.

"We're not that different. We're both single."

"I'm amazed you are, Brett. What happened to Tessa?" Tessa O'Brien had been his girlfriend when he was a teenager. O'Brien's Farm was about equal to Stanton Farm in class. A merger between the two families would have been good news.

Brett raised an eyebrow. "You remember who my girlfriend was?"

She shouldn't have mentioned Tessa. Now it seemed as if she had dwelled on his life. "Oh, I just recalled you used to go out with her. Didn't you?"

"Yes, I did. But we broke up before I went to college. She married someone else a few years ago. And we certainly weren't compatible. I'm too close to the land for Tessa. Tessa prefers the peripheral social whirl that horse breeding, er, breeds."

Kim fiddled with her spoon. "And you don't?"

"Not particularly, Kim. I'm a down-home country boy at heart." He spoke the last words with an exaggerated drawl.

"Wow," she said, putting on an exaggerated drawl herself. "You do surprise me, Brett. I thought for sure you were a socializer."

"I can socialize with the best of them if I have to, but I would rather be riding a horse. You used to ride, didn't you?"

"Yes, I did. My uncle owned a riding stable." Her uncle was dead now, so she wouldn't be riding there. She hadn't ridden for a long time, except on a vacation in Barbados, when she had given in to passion and gone for a horse ride with a friend.

"We have a solid stable of riding horses, Kim."

Of course they would, wouldn't they, she thought cynically.

"You're welcome to come and ride at the farm."

She might just do that. The exercise would

help to release the tension inside her. Besides, she had never ridden any of the Stanton's beautiful horses. Maybe, after all, there would be some perks to her sister marrying a Stanton. It would certainly put the Russell family on the right side of the fence in Valleyview.

"Do you want to ride?"

"Yes. That would be nice. Thank you."

"Then I'll arrange it."

Snap your fingers. Brett. Magic. Everything so easy for a Stanton.

Brett drained the rest of his coffee and noticed Kim had finished hers. "Ready to face the music now?"

"Only if it's in tune."

He leaned forward and said softly, "Make it be in tune, Kim. I won't tell anyone anything. Your mother obviously hasn't. You obviously haven't. My father's never said a word."

Kim turned cold. He did remember. "I'm not sure what . . ."

"Yes you are. It's probably half the reason why you don't want to get back to Valleyview in a hurry. Josie said you hadn't been home for nearly three years. They've been to visit you instead."

"They like to come to Chicago, and I give them a place to stay."

"I'm sure they do, but you could come home once in a while as well."

"I don't get much vacation."

"Who is arguing now?" he asked. "Look. We both remember what happened, but it's over and done with a long time ago."

"Then you do admit it's an awkward situa tion?"

"Only if you make it awkward."

His eyes glittered as he looked at her. Kim drew in a breath. He was more than merely attractive. He emanated power. She swallowed hard to try and eliminate his spell. "I'm trying to forget it happened." Kim lifted her purse from the seat.

Brett extracted dollar bills from his wallet and picked up the check with the money. "It is our parents' problem. It's not up to us to make waves."

"Have there already been undercurrents?"

"I was obviously watching at first. And I did think your mother and my father were a little edgy with one another. But I don't think anyone else noticed."

"I'll notice?"

"Makes sense you probably will. But if they're handling it, then don't have an anxiety attack about it. You stay with me. I'll be your escort at the wedding."

"So what are you saying? That you'll put a lid on me, on everything?"

He smiled at her and rose from his seat. "That's a good enough description, I guess. But in my opinion, it just puts all the problems in one corner, so nothing can escape. You want it that way, I'll make sure it stays that way."

Glaring at his black leather back, Kim followed him and stood aside as he paid the bill. Listening to him flirt with the cashier made her turn and walk through the door without him. She drew in some gasping breaths of cool air. She knew she wouldn't be content again until she was on the plane back to Chicago.

Chapter Two

Brett drove past gas stations and fast food restaurants on the way back to the Interstate. He seemed serious. Therefore, Kim was surprised when he suddenly chuckled.

"You need to kick back a little, Kim. You're in some type of city straightjacket of your own making. It'll do you good to let loose at the wedding."

She stared at him. "You don't know anything about me."

His eyes twinkled. "Nothing I won't find out over the next week."

Whoa. This was another side of Brett. A charming side. "A week isn't that long," she said shakily.

"Long enough." He maneuvered the return ramp to the busy Interstate. Once the vehicle was gliding smoothly along the freeway, he moved restlessly in his seat, adjusting his body and long muscular legs until he was comfortable.

Kim looked away. To get involved with him would be a recipe for disaster. She didn't want anything in Valleyview with the power to pull her back home. Her own family was enough. Except, soon the Stantons would also be part of that family. What was she going to do in the future? She had stayed away for three years, mainly because her vacation times had been sporadic and her family enjoyed a chance to get to Chicago. But she would have to begin returning to Valleyview more often. And how would she survive those tumultuous trips, which now would include the Stanton family?

Brett left the freeway and drove along country roads that wound through fields of pure green. Smooth-coated well-bred horses grazed between miles of pristine white fences. Then landmarks of Valleyview came into view. The brick high school on the edge of town, an old massive tree demolished to build a new extension wing. Then the neat tree-shaded streets with rows of small houses. The wooden general store, the white-washed church with its towering spire, a pottery, a framing shop, and Bookmarks, the bookstore owned by Kim's friend Gina and her husband, Tom. Their wedding had been the first Kim had ever attended. Gina and Tom had been high school sweethearts and married as soon as they graduated.

A homestead had been made into an inn, with a sign that advertised Bed & Breakfast and good dining. That was new in the years since Kim had been back. Not far from the B&B was Russell's, from where her grandfather, and later her father, ran the family blacksmith business. It was a blue-sided two-story building. A miniature anvil and horseshoes hung as decoration around the eaves of the porch. In her grandfather's day it was told that customers had once gathered there to chat about their horses, partake of village gossip, or ruminate on a good race bet. Little actual farrier work was done on the premises now, so the yard out back had become a garden of the pots containing her mother's flowers. The family lived in the rest of the house. A far cry from the sprawling acres of Stanton Farm.

Brett stopped at the side in the gravel parking area near her family's cars. Kim let out a breath. Was she uptight about seeing her own parents and her sister, or was she uptight because of Brett being here with her to see where she lived?

Silly, she scolded herself. *He knows where you live. What does it matter?* It was just that the circumstances weren't normal. On the weekend, the Russell family and the Stanton family would be united in matrimony. And it had never been normal for Brett Stanton to drive her home.

Brett carried her luggage to the porch, but he didn't put it down.

"I'll carry it in," he said.

She didn't really want him inside. "You can leave it there."

"Open the door, Kim."

Reluctantly, Kim opened the door and called out, "Mom. I'm home." The way she always had.

Brett came right into the narrow little hallway behind her. It was so unlike the huge foyer of Stanton Farm that Kim felt embarrassed. He moved past her to place her bags at the base of the stairs and stood back close to her. Kim's heart was beating erratically, palpitating. She knew then that most of her panic was caused by Brett. She couldn't have forgotten his smiles, or his teasing remarks when she had been sixteen. She remembered now watching him one time from an upstairs bedroom window at Stanton Farm, when she really should have been dusting the furniture. He had been wearing a denim jacket and jeans. He walked, even then, with a long masculine stride. And she remembered she had experienced a tilt to her heart that she had never experienced when watching a man since.

Kim was thankful to see her mother come to greet her from the back of the house. Moira was an attractive woman in her early fifties with very short, fashionable dark hair. Her blue eyes met Kim's, and Kim was sure they cautioned her that their secret was still a secret. Except Brett remembers, Kim thought. She wondered if her mother recalled that Brett had been around that evening.

Moira said hello to Brett, then hugged her daughter and held her at arm's length. "You look great, honey. What a smart suit."

"She looks like a big city office worker," Brett drawled.

Josie, her long golden hair in a braid, wearing jeans and a soft white silk blouse, bounced down the stairs. "Hey, Kimmy. Brett, hi."

Brett grinned at her. "Hi, sister-in-law-to-be. Where's my brother?"

"He went home about half an hour ago. He's coming to pick us up tonight and we're all going to the farm. It's sort of a welcome home and a get-to-know-one-another for Kim."

Kim didn't need this. She looked at her mother, but Moira glanced away and spoke to the air.

"Your dad will be home shortly. He had some work at O'Brien's today."

Kim bit back a remark about the wealthy still keeping Allan Russell hopping. She was going to have to watch her tongue and behave herself.

"So I'll see you all tonight," Brett said. "Take it easy," he said to Kim personally. He kissed Josie's cheek and went to the front door.

They all gathered on the porch with Brett. He strolled away in the rather insolent manner that had so fascinated Kim years ago. She kept her eyes fastened on him as he climbed into his four-wheel-drive, turned it around, and roared away with a salute out the window. She saw him like a proud animal. And he had every right to be. He was the best of family stock.

"Look at my ring," Josie said, thrusting her hand forward. "What do you think?"

Kim dragged her eyes away from Brett's brake lights and took hold of her sister's slim fingers. The diamond, surrounded by smaller diamonds in a daisy arrangement, winked at her. "It's beautiful, Josie."

"But?" Josie asked, looking up the road that was now empty of traffic. "What happened with Brett?"

"Nothing," Kim said quickly. She had to snap

out of the past. The present was all that counted. "Everything was cool."

"Then why do you look so anxious?"

"I'm tired, not anxious. I had an early morning, getting to the airport."

"Flying is exhausting," Moira said. "Let Kim get settled in, Josie."

Josie let out a big sigh. "See. I still get treated like a little kid around here. Things will change when I'm married."

"Josie," Moira said firmly, "behave yourself. If you act like a mature young woman, I'll treat you like one. Now let's get back inside and take Kimberley's luggage upstairs."

Josie made faces as Moira headed indoors. Kim laughed. Josie and Moira were always at odds. Moira liked to keep decorum in the home, and Josie was a little wild at times. However, it was better being home than Kim had thought it would be. Brett had caused a lot of her tension. Now that he was gone for a while, she could relax.

Her room was still painted pale blue. Her childhood furniture, also pale blue, was edged by painted flowers around the drawers. A quilt with masses of colorful flowers was new.

"I bought this for you," Josie said, stroking it. "Do you like it? Your old one went to the cat."

"Cat?" Kim said.

"We have a kitten," her mother told her. "Her name is Purr."

"Original," Kim commented, tossing her carry-on onto the bed. "The quilt is lovely, Josie. Thank you."

Josie tucked Kim's suitcase against the closet. "The kitten is for Mom, because she'll be lonely when I leave, and with you in Chicago."

"It's a good idea. Does Dad like cats?"

"Not particularly," Moira said. "But right now he's outnumbered. Now I'm going to fix some lunch. I've got a chicken casserole in the oven."

Moira left Kim's room and went downstairs. Josie grimaced. "She's not that cool about the wedding, Kim."

Kim unbuttoned her jacket. "Well, you are her youngest daughter. She's probably upset about letting you go."

"She never minded you going to Chicago."

"She probably did, Josie—she just didn't get in the way of my progress."

"I suppose. But she's like you, she's dead against the Stanton family. I don't know why. They never did anything but be wealthy."

"No. They didn't," Kim said carefully, and touched her sister's arm. "Don't worry. Everything will be fine."

"I sure hope so. We had a big argument the other night. I finally had to lay it on the line with her, Kim. I love Brand. Brand loves me. And the wedding is going to happen. She'll have to come to terms with it. Although, she has fitted her dress and everything, so she's not planning on opting out altogether. She's just acting weird."

"She'll be there, Josie. Don't worry, Mom won't let you down. How about my dress?"

"I showed the dressmaker a photograph of you and gave her your measurements. Tomorrow afternoon we'll go and finalize all that stuff. My dress is finished already. It's absolutely gorgeous. And I hope you like yours."

"I will. Don't worry," Kim said, trying to make herself sound light-hearted. She couldn't let Josie down. And neither could their mother. She had yet to witness her father's reaction. Maybe being home wasn't so great after all.

Kim changed into white leggings and a long navy T-shirt to have the meal her mother had prepared. Purr, an eight-month-old black and white female cat, kept a vigil beneath the kitchen table for scraps. Allan Russell, slim with brown hair, looking more haggard than his sixty years warranted, worked long, hard hours to keep the family going. Moira hadn't worked full-time since the Stanton dismissal. There had been medical problems with grandparents that kept the family poor for a while. But Kim and Josie had both helped with part-time jobs. College hadn't been denied them, even if Josie had quit during her second year toward a law degree for a well-paying job with a local lawyer.

"Mother is working again now," Allan said as he sampled his lunch.

"Where, Mom?" Kim asked.

Moira served herself some salad. "Down at the supermarket. Just part-time."

Kim frowned. "Do you need to?"

"No, she doesn't," her father said. "I've had to hire two men to help me lately. I'm getting a lot of business."

"That's great, Dad. So you don't have to work quite so hard now?"

"No. And I'm feeling better for it as well. Being a boss suits me."

Kim glanced around the table. "That's great. Isn't it? So why are you working, Mom?"

"I like to work," her mother said. "There's always extras needed. Like going up to Chicago to visit you."

"You don't come home very often anymore, Kim," her father said.

"No, I know. I'll come home more in the future. My vacation time goes up next year." And with the promotion she would get even more.

"I hope so," Allan told her. "Anyway, this brings us to the reason you're here, Kim. What do you think of Josie marrying into that family, Kim?"

"Impressive," Kim said, ignoring his emphasis on *that family*.

Josie glanced down at her picked-over meal. "Don't call them 'that family.' Brand is going to be my husband."

"We know, Josie. Shush," Moira said.

Kim felt sorry for Josie, and she wondered if they should have been more open and honest about Moira's dismissal. If Josie had known, she might never have given into Brand's attentions, and the wedding might not be happening. Allan certainly wouldn't stand for it, if he'd known.

The women dressed up for the evening, Moira in a plain black dress with pearls around her neck and Kim in a green silk suit with a short skirt. She slipped her feet into matching high heels and added a pair of small gold earrings, intent on keeping up her big city appearance. Josie put on a white dress with a navy jacket, her hair no longer braided but loose and crimped. She crimped Kim's brilliant copper hair as well and told her sister it made her look softer. Kim had to agree, although she wasn't sure she wanted to appear soft in front of Brett.

Allan had put on his best dark blue suit and looked stiff and uncomfortable. Kim hated the way they all stood on the porch waiting until Brand came by in a silver-gray Mercedes sedan displaying a Stanton *S* on the license plate. Kim thought the neighbors must be eyeing them with raised brows. She was just thankful no one in town had known about her mother's dismissal that night. Moira wouldn't have been able to hold her head up high for the rest of her life if the fight with Frank Stanton had become public knowledge. Kim now understood why the incident had to be kept secret forever.

Brand, wearing a dark suit and a navy shirt, greeted Josie with a long kiss and shook everyone else's hands. Brett but not quite Brett, Kim thought, sitting in the back seat of the luxury car with her mom and dad. Brand had less character in his more youthful features, and his hair was a lighter brown. It was longer as well and rested on his jacket collar. However, he smiled a lot and teased Josie in a playful way. They seemed perfect for one another on the surface. Kim desperately hoped everything would go fine in the years to come, and that the families would meld, or at least stay cordial.

Stanton Farm was a few miles outside the town, but Brand drove quite fast and soon turned the car past sturdy stone posts and onto the asphalted road that led to a circular driveway. As he slowed and parked, Kim looked at the house. The bricks on the hundred-year-old house had been repointed to preserve its excellent condition. Two white round columns flanked the porch, and the windows had dark green shutters either side of them, a nice complement to the sloping manicured lawns and neatly trimmed hedges and shrubs. All the outbuildings were topped with cupolas, their spires high enough to be shrouded by a light mist. Rail fences edged the fields to the horizon.

Brand opened the door for them and led them into the stone-floored foyer with its forest of potted tropical ferns. The rest of the Stanton family appeared from the same sitting room Kim's mother had run from that fateful evening. Frank had thick silver hair and wore an immaculate black suit. Liz, his small, rather plain wife, wore a mauve silk dress, and Kim didn't think her short brown hairstyle was very fashionable. In Kim's estimation Moira was much more attractive. Remembering Brett's comment on how aware they were of one another, she watched how Frank shook her mother's hand and greeted her. She thought Frank seemed quite struck by her mother's appearance, which was strange, because Frank had treated Moira like dirt, and Kim thought he would dislike her.

Brett was the only man not wearing a suit. But his dark pants and white silky shirt did nothing to detract from his powerful body. Or his attraction, Kim thought as he held her hand too many seconds more than she felt were required.

Frank Stanton summoned them—the way it felt to Kim—into the sitting room. The glass doors at one end of the room looked out onto a big patio and the gardens, with darkness settling upon them. Bottles of champagne were poured into crystal glasses and served by two maids in black and white uniforms.

Josie jabbed Kim in the thigh with a finger. "Impressive?"

Kim grinned. "You sure you'll like it?"

"Would you?"

"I suppose I could get used to it."

"We'll have our own place anyway."

Brett stepped forward with his glass in his hand. "Let's toast the happy couple." He raised his glass. "To Josie and Brand: a very long, prosperous, happy life together. Best wishes."

Kim drank her toast, looking at Josie and Brand kissing. Brand did seem truly mesmerized with her lovely sister. Kim wondered for a moment if a man would ever look at her with such a soft glow in his eyes. Then Kim glanced at Brett, who was talking to her mother and father. Would he ever find the woman to light his fire?

Turning away from the scene, Kim pretended to peruse in detail some of the paintings on the wall. They were a collection of old masters, and some were probably worth a fortune. She noticed there was a security system hooked up to them.

Someone touched her arm, and she knew it was Brett. No one else's firm touch made her body tingle with awareness.

"All right?" he asked softly, bending low so only she heard the whisper. The brush of his breath against her ear ruffled her hair, and she inhaled the aroma of musky aftershave.

She kept her stare pinned on a pink rose petal in an oil painting. "Shouldn't I be?"

His fingers curved more firmly around her elbow. It felt right for him to touch her that way, and she was disgusted with herself, because she didn't want anything about Brett to feel right. She stiffened her body, her breathing on hold, as if waiting for something catastrophic to happen.

"I sense you're still as edgy as when I met you."

She could still feel his breath raising her hair. "I'm a hyperactive city dweller," she commented.

"Except you're on vacation for a week. Come for a horse ride first thing in the morning. I'll pick you up from home around six."

"I don't think so, Brett."

"I thought you wanted to ride again."

"I do."

"First thing in the morning is the best time."

Kim lifted her glass to her lips. "Why would you want to take me?"

"Because I promised to take you riding, didn't I?" His hand holding his glass brushed her hair aside.

Kim swallowed hard to stop his touch from bothering her, met his gaze, and drowned in it. "I don't know if you promised to take me, or if I was just going to ride your horses."

Brett moved his head forward slightly, almost as if he were going to kiss her. "You won't be able to ride from our stables without my permission. And you might be too busy after tomorrow. It makes sense I introduce you to the stables right away." He squeezed her elbow. "I'll look forward to the ride."

He left her alone then, and she stared at his back as he went over to talk to Josie and Brand. She heard him chuckle at something Josie said and she returned her eyes to the paintings, but she wasn't really interested. She had just made arrangements to ride with Brett tomorrow morning and she wished she didn't feel so excited about it.

Needing a break, she edged out of the sitting room and tried to remember where the bathrooms were. She knew there was one upstairs, so she climbed the big staircase, occasionally glancing down at the foyer. Nothing had really changed in the past ten years. The house was still elegant, with an old-fashioned feel to it.

However, the bathrooms were all large and renovated to include either showers or whirlpool baths. She brushed her hair, wishing that Josie hadn't fixed it into flowing waves. She preferred her hair upswept because it made her feel more sophisticated. With her hair flowing all over her shoulders, she felt wild and uncontrolled. Unable to do much about it, she left the bathroom and idly glanced into some of the rooms as she made her way to the stairs. She came to the bedroom where her mother had accidentally burned the piece of furniture. As far as she knew the oak dresser was still the same one. She remembered it had those clawed feet.

Glancing around to see if she was alone, Kim walked in and tossed her purse onto the bed. She ran her fingers across the top of the dresser but she couldn't feel a burn mark, or see one. She went back to the wall and turned on the light. She still couldn't see anything. She narrowed her eyes. No. Nothing. Maybe they'd had it repaired. She wondered who they thought had burned the surface.

"What are you doing?"

Kim jumped to her feet and twisted around. Brett leaned against the doorpost, his arms folded.

"Oh, just checking my appearance in the mirror."

One of his eyebrows rose. "Hunkered down like that?"

"I dropped something." She quickly scrambled in her mind for something. "An eyeliner pencil."

He loosened his arms, straightened, and walked into the room, looking down at the thick cream carpet. "Did you find it?"

"Oh, yes. I did. Thanks."

"Then where is it?"

"Oh. In my purse.

"I didn't see you put it in your purse. Your purse is on the bed. My bed, by the way."

"This is your room?" Kim frowned. "It wasn't always."

"No. But I wanted to move into the back of

the house, so I switched with my parents since they are leaving soon."

"Well, this is a nice room." Kim glanced around her. "You kept the same furniture?"

"No, I moved my own in. That dresser is the same one, though. I'll be moving that out soon to make room for something else I need in here."

"Great." Kim smiled.

Brett also smiled. "So shall we look for that eyeliner pencil?"

"It's okay. I . . . found it." She grabbed her purse from *his* bed. "Really I did."

"Then let's go downstairs again. We're going to be served a buffet supper."

Kim walked downstairs again with Brett beside her this time. She really did want to ask if the dresser had been refinished, but she didn't want to bring up the subject of their parents.

A buffet meal was set out in a big room with hardwood floors. Small tables and chairs were set around. Kim found herself with Brett and Brand and Josie, while their parents sat at another table. She remembered her mother polishing this floor with a floor polisher.

Brand said, "I'm not sure if I remember ever meeting you before, Kim."

"She used to come here to work with Mom," Josie said.

"She did? I wasn't very old, was I?"

"You were probably about fourteen," Brett said and glanced at Kim. "I remember her."

Kim nibbled a piece of celery. "I didn't come here all the time. I don't think you were around much, Brand. Probably out with the horses. We came after school."

"Maybe that's why I never met you. I rode each day after school." Brand smiled.

Thinking he was very handsome, Kim returned his smile. So it was all common knowledge that her mother used to work here. Was her dismissal also common knowledge in the Stanton family? Were they secretly sniggering behind Moira's back?

Kim found the evening hard going. Not only was she tense, she was also beginning to feel tired from all the traveling. By the end of the meal she could barely keep her eyes open. She sensed Brett watching her.

"What?" she asked.

"You look tired."

"I am," she admitted.

"Shall I run you home?"

"No. I'll wait."

"No. I'll take you home. You look dead on your feet."

"Brett, I'm fine."

"You don't look fine."

"I'm fine," she said defiantly. "Josie arranged this for me to get together with your family. I can't run out on her."

"All right, but if you feel you need to go home, let me know."

As it turned out, the evening didn't last much longer. When she was with Josie, while Brand was bringing the car to the door, she whispered, "I didn't think Brand knew mother worked here."

"Of course he does."

"Is he okay with it?"

"Of course he is." Josie shook her head in amazement that Kim would still be going on about the subject.

Kim sat in the back seat with her parents again. She glanced at her mother and thought Moira appeared a little tense around the mouth. Kim didn't mention the early morning ride with Brett to her family. She wondered what would happen if she didn't go with him. But then, what would that accomplish but to cause even more family tension?

Chapter Three

Knowing what was to come in the morning, Kim tossed and turned all night. She got up early to rifle through her closet for some old clothes. She found ancient jeans, a dark green sweatshirt with a horse embroidered on the front, a denim jacket, and an old pair of leather riding boots. She tied back her hair with a black velvet bow and was tucking a pair of leather riding gloves into her pocket, when she heard a car pull up. She pulled back the curtains at the window and saw Brett's black vehicle by the curb. He looked up and she waved. Her mother had left her a front door key on her dressing table, so she tucked it into a small wallet and stuffed it into the jacket pocket. Then she tiptoed down the stairs and out into the damp misty air.

Brett leaned against the passenger door, his fingers jammed in the front pockets of supple tight jeans worn with his western boots, a gray hooded sweatshirt, and a denim jacket. His hair was carelessly tousled, his jaw unshaven, but he still looked superb.

He moved forward, his hands sliding from his pockets to Kim's hips. "Ah, you look good in those clothes."

She held her breath. If she didn't, she might explode at his closeness. She spoke tautly. "I dug them out my closet."

He raised an eyebrow and patted her hips. "A little baggy there. Have you lost weight? You're not on one of those stupid diets, are you?"

"No. I'm not on a diet, but I like to keep slim and fit. And I never have time to eat lunch."

"That's the most ridiculous thing I've ever heard. I'll take you for lunch one day. How about tomorrow?"

"Let's get through the ride first," Kim told him, and eased away from his possessive grip.

"I had this feeling you might stand me up," Brett said as he drove through the empty town, one arm on the rolled down window, one hand on the steering wheel.

The misty cool air touched her skin. "I thought I might, but I decided added tension wasn't what we needed." Not that she wasn't experiencing added tension. She could still feel the pressure of his hands on her hips.

He gave her a look. "Tension between men and women usually translates to attraction."

"Key word, *usually*," she retorted. "Besides, I wasn't saying the tension was between you and me."

"Oh? You're talking about that, are you? Well . . ." He grinned. "You can relax, Kim. I'm not going to jump up during the wedding ceremony and scream obscenities, and I'm not going to stop my brother from marrying your sister."

"That's a relief, I suppose. What about your father?"

"He hasn't said anything."

"You haven't asked him if, well, firing my mother from her job, bothered him?"

"No, I don't want to go there with him. All right?"

"I understand. I don't really want to talk to my mother either. I'd like to let it go."

"Me, too. Therefore, let's forget it. If our parents aren't having a fit, then it's not up to us to question the situation."

Kim sighed. He was probably right. But she knew her mother was questioning it all. If Josie was right about the arguments with Mom, Moira was having a fit.

Brett continued, "It's none of our business really. It's certainly nothing to do with Brand and Josie. My parents will be moving away after the wedding and everything will be fine, I'm sure."

"In other words, you're just brushing the past under the carpet?"

"You could say that. Although I'd like to think of it as keeping the peace."

"But Brand knows my mother worked at your house."

"Of course he does. He knew her. But he truly couldn't remember you."

"But you did."

"Oh, Kim. I'm four years older than Brand. Naturally I would remember you. You remembered me, didn't you?"

"Yes," she said. "I remembered you."

"Well, then. Change the subject. It's over and done with and it doesn't pertain to this wedding. Let's get back to us. Did you really find your pencil or whatever you dropped last night? I looked but didn't see anything."

"I told you I did, Brett. I was also looking to see if the dresser had been refinished."

He frowned. "You mean stripped and revarnished?"

"Yes. It seemed very beautiful for its age."

"I didn't know you had an interest in antiques. Although you seemed very attached to the paintings in the sitting room."

"I'm interested in a lot of different things," she said.

"That's fine. We have fascinating pieces around the farm, some of them going back a generation or two. As a matter of fact, we did have the top refinished. I can't recall exactly, but I know something happened to it and it needed work."

Kim was pleased the mark had been repaired to retain the value of the furniture. Her relief that Moira's cigarette burn wasn't there anymore was so great—almost like a burden lifted—that she was reminded of Josie's remark about her never being able to let anything go.

And it's probably the truth, Kim decided as she looked out at the passing scenery. Mist rolled over the fields. Houses were silent. But there were lights burning in the barns. The horses were being tended to. She began to look forward to the upcoming ride as they turned through the gates of Stanton Farm.

Instead of going to the house, Brett negotiated the twisting narrow road on the property, until he reached a low stone building that housed the riding stables. The breeding stables were set apart. Kim had never actually visited any of the horse facilities at Stanton Farm, and she felt her heart pound with excited anticipation as she walked into the warm musky atmosphere of the stables and saw the beautiful horses being tended to by grooms and handlers. She inhaled the scent of the sweet hay.

"Memories, Kim," Brett murmured.

She met his gaze and she knew he knew that she missed it here. "Yes," she admitted.

He touched her shoulder. "It's okay to want to be in two places at once."

"How do you know this?"

"Because I can tell you're mixed up. You love your big-city life, but your heart is really here."

"It probably will have to stay that way forever, Brett."

"Possibly, but you can enjoy this, can't you? I mean, you don't have to think of the future. Live for today."

He was right. She smiled at him through sudden tears.

He bent his head slightly, and she felt a moment of anticipation. Then a voice interrupted them.

"Hi, Brett. I've saddled Princess for your guest

and Ranger's ready for you." A sturdily built blond-haired man came over to them.

Brett turned around. "Thank you, Don. Don Harrison, this is Kim Russell. Josie's sister. Kim, Don manages the riding stables. If you want a ride, when you're here, just come down to the stables and talk to Don."

"You do that, Kim," Don said, shaking Kim's hand with a pumping action. "Nice to meet you. Here for the wedding?"

"Yes," Kim said with a smile. "I live in Chicago and don't get to ride much anymore, so Brett has kindly given me a chance."

"That's great. I hope you enjoy your ride today."

Don left the barn and Brett led Kim outside, where their mounts were already tethered, groomed, and waiting. Princess was a Palomino with a fluffy cream tail.

"She's beautiful, Brett," Kim said, as she stroked the horse's fine honey coat, and they nuzzled one another. When she looked back at Brett he was gazing at her intently.

"Remember how to jump on board?" he said huskily.

"Of course." Kim eased on her leather gloves, walked around Princess, drew in a deep breath, let it out, and mounted efficiently. Feeling exu-

berant because she hadn't fallen head-first across
the horse in front of Brett, she adjusted the reins.

Brett smiled and prodded the stirrup more
firmly beneath her foot. "Nice seat."

Kim ignored him and tossed her head. Was that
flirting?

Brett mounted his own big black horse,
Ranger.

Kim thought he looked natural on the horse.
The same way he looked natural driving his four-
wheel-drive, or receiving company and toasting
the bride and groom last evening. She walked
Princess up beside Ranger. The two horses butted
one another. Princess reared back slightly. Experiencing a rush of adrenaline, Kim brought the
horse under control.

"You haven't lost your touch?"

"It doesn't seem like it." He had never seen
her ride, so he really didn't know what her touch
had been in the past.

"Don't worry about the two horses. They often
ride together."

"But not with me on the back of Princess.
She's used to someone else. Who?"

He passed her a veiled look. "Stephanie."

Kim ignored a rush of jealousy and rode forward. "Your girlfriend?"

He moved his horse up beside hers. "A very special one."

"I didn't think you had anyone special. You gave me the impression no one had ever . . . lit your fire."

"Ah, this little girl has. She's my ten-year-old niece."

Kim felt like a fool. She had forgotten there was another Stanton sibling—Deanna, his sister, who had married Gordon Fishburn from Fishburn Farms. "I didn't think."

He chuckled. "Good. Because I loved the reaction."

Kim gritted her teeth. She was going to have to act cooler around Brett, and think before she reacted. The last thing she needed was to have Brett think she was falling in love with him. What better way to be taken advantage of by a Stanton?

"Anyway," Brett said as they began to walk the horses side by side. "Stephie might be ten, but acts thirty, and she rides like a charm because she's been on the back of a horse all of her life. She says she wants to be a jockey."

"Really?"

Brett nodded. "If she doesn't sprout up tall like her mother. But her father's short. Gord's brother, Freddy, is a jockey."

"I don't follow horse racing," Kim admitted.

And it wasn't because she didn't enjoy watching it on TV or going to the races, but because if she did, she would feel that pang of yearning, and it was better she never gave in to those urges.

Brett gave her a steady look. "Why are you denying that side of yourself, Kim?"

"I'm not denying it," she fibbed. "I'm just not interested anymore."

"Yet you're an expert horsewoman."

"I'm not expert. I'm okay. I learned to ride when I was very young."

"It's in your blood, Kim. But I guess city life must keep you buzzing."

"It does," she told him firmly. "I don't miss all this, really." But she did. Oh, she did.

They had reached the edge of a field. Beyond them was scenery designed for a ride in a million, and her heart cramped. She glanced at Brett before they began their ride and she saw him looking at her with a mixture of understanding and triumph in his eyes.

Princess was an easy ride. She responded to Kim's hands over the gorgeous scenery of Stanton Farm, which consisted of trails through the woods, open fields, and panoramic views from the tops of hills. By the time they arrived back at the stables, Kim felt exhilarated from a gallop over the Stanton acres.

"Great," she called out, laughing with pleasure. She had been surprised when Brett didn't try to beat her, but had paced his horse beside her. She would have expected Brett to be the type of person who always wanted to win, but then she decided Brett probably didn't feel a need to win, because he had been born at the top.

"You are a good rider, Kim. Don't underestimate yourself."

Her skin was flushed from the exertion so it didn't matter if another rush of pleasure put a blush to her cheeks. "Well, I knew I was," she said modestly.

He grinned. "We could do this every morning while you're here."

"I'm not sure, Brett. Josie needs me for things."

"I know, but if you want to ride, just come over here alone. Okay?"

"Okay. Thanks."

They dismounted and a groom came to take the horses for brushing.

Kim was just getting her land feet when she felt a strong hand on her shoulder. "Let's go for coffee," Brett said, leading her from the stable.

Beneath the pressure of his hand on her shoulder, Kim breathed deeply. A weak sun showed in the sky and the air was warming up. She thought of her family beginning to get up in the house. "I think I should get back."

"Not without coffee and a muffin. We have a cook who makes the most delicious muffins each morning."

A cook! "I'm fine, Brett."

He stopped walking and drew her around to face him. His fingers still gripped her shoulder. "You have to eat. So relax and come and eat. Don't fight me all the time. You need to let go and enjoy yourself. We're going to be your family now."

Kim raised her eyes to the silvery sky. One moment he flirted, the next he was earnestly letting her know he was family. She wasn't quite sure which corner he was coming from. She told the truth. "I don't want to be involved with your family."

"Well, you are involved with my family, like it or not," he almost growled at her. "My brother and your sister are getting married on Saturday. You and I will be related in some respects." His green eyes flashed.

"We don't have to see one another," she said with a toss of her head, trying to wriggle away from his hand.

"We'll see one another. You think Josie won't want to see you? She'll be living here."

Kim let out a breath to calm herself, but she didn't feel any calmer. Brett's fingers on her shoulder had now turned caressing. Warmth flowed through her. She noticed he was breathing heavier as well.

"Please. Come and have some coffee," he said firmly. "At least let me have a cup before I drive you home."

What could she do? By next week she would be back in Chicago, far away from Valleyview. If she remembered that, she would be fine.

"Okay." She gave in.

Brett let go of her shoulder and walked in front of her. Kim followed, feeling she was getting far too intertwined with him.

Nancy was about thirty, with a gourmet cooking degree. Her muffins were low in fat and filled with fruit. Kim surprised herself by eating two and drinking two cups of the delicious coffee.

She was sitting at the kitchen table with Brett when Brett's mother, wearing English riding gear, came into the kitchen.

"Hi, you two," Liz said, accepting a glass of orange juice from Nancy. "Did you ride already?"

"We did," Brett said. "Kim hasn't ridden for a while, so I thought this would be a chance to get her back into the saddle."

"Of course. Come over anytime, Kim. I'll ride

with you if Brett isn't available. Frank doesn't pleasure ride much any more. And Deanna's been busy starting her framing shop in town." Liz smiled widely. "Anyway, I'll go have my little ride now. Nice seeing you again, Kim."

Kim nodded. "Yes, Mrs. Stanton."

"Call me Liz. Please."

The door shuddered behind Brett's mother. Kim put her coffee mug on the table. "We should have waited for your mother."

"She likes to ride alone."

"It didn't sound like it." Kim thought Liz Stanton had seemed lonely.

Brett rubbed his neck. "It's okay, Kim. Really. I don't know from one day to the next when she is going to ride."

"Do you ever ride with her?"

"Sometimes. Mainly I take Stephanie out. Mother takes Stephanie out as well."

Kim wondered if Liz had ever known about that evening. She must have been puzzled as to why Moira had left so suddenly. Oh dear, the Stanton family did exhaust her. She looked at her watch. "I should get home."

Brett rose from the table and shrugged into his jacket. He pulled his keys from the pocket. "Okay. Come on."

He seemed cooler with her now, as if he had

a lot on his mind. He dropped her off with no mention of another outing. Obviously he's forgotten lunch tomorrow, she thought as she pushed her key into the front door lock.

Kim knew she had stayed away too long. Her mother was up and came into the hallway to greet her. Purr rubbed around Kim's legs. Kim picked the cat up in her arms and nuzzled the velvety head.

"Where have you been?" Moira asked.

Purr sniffed a strand of hay on the sleeve of Kim's denim jacket. "Riding with Brett."

"Don't you get involved with one of them as well, Kim."

"I'm not. I just went riding." Kim followed her mother into the kitchen, where coffee was dripping into a carafe. She watched her mother set the table with placemats and cutlery. "It's a problem for you, Josie marrying Brand, isn't it?"

Her mother looked at her. "You know it is. It's very difficult, but I don't want anything said. I want Josie happy."

Purr jumped onto a chair and Kim eased off her denim jacket. "Brand remembers you were the housekeeper, though."

"Maybe, but he wasn't around much."

"Brett was."

Her mother gave her a sharp glance. "Have you two been discussing it?"

"Not really discussing it. But we know we know."

"Yes. Well. He's a nice man. I think he can be trusted not to say anything to Josie. And not a word from you, Kim. Not a word."

Kim zipped her mouth with her finger. "Lips sealed. They always have been."

But she felt heavy-footed as she walked upstairs to her room to change her clothes. She stripped off her riding gear, which smelled of sweat and horses. She hadn't smelled like this for a long time. She hadn't felt quite the way she had this morning for a long time either. For a few moments, when she had been out with Brett in the fields, she had felt truly free of a lot of burdens she had carried throughout her life.

And yet she'd been with Brett, she thought, as she stood under the shower, pampering herself with moisturizing body wash. Why would being with Brett give her a sense of freedom?

Kim went with Josie in Josie's car to fit their dresses that afternoon.

"Where did you go this morning?" Josie asked, turning her white car into the driveway of a new brick house. FABULOUS FASHION WEDDINGS were advertised on a sign.

"How did you know I went anywhere?"

"I heard the front door open and close. And then I heard you come back and you were talking to Mom."

Nothing was secret in the Russell household. Kim was amazed at the secret she and her mother had managed to keep.

Kim told the truth. "I went riding with Brett."

Josie gave her a quick glance. "Whoo hoo. I thought yesterday there was something burning, and I smelled smoke. I watched how he kept staring at you last night."

"He kept staring at me?"

Josie nodded. "Yes. But he was talking to you for quite a long time as well. So you should know. I thought you two seemed very intimate. Then when you disappeared, he followed and you were gone a long time."

Kim didn't think she had been under such close surveillance. But she remembered the brush of Brett's fingers, the way his breath ruffled her hair. "Nothing happened much, other than he asked me to go riding with him. That's all."

"That's all? Brett's passion is riding. If he shares his passion with a woman, it means something." Josie turned off the engine and withdrew the key. "I can understand why he would like you. You're really beautiful. Don't you think he's a sweetie, Kim?"

Kim rolled her eyes. "The word sweetie doesn't exactly describe Brett. He's quite hard-nosed."

"Well, yeah, but only because he's got the entire responsibility of the farm on his shoulders."

"Doesn't Brand help?"

"Of course he does. But Brett will be mostly responsible.

And he doesn't take his responsibilities lightly. I told you he was like you. He gets heavy."

"Am I really heavy, Josie?"

"Yes, you are. I think it would be great if you did fall in love with Brett. Not only would you find love like I have, but we'd be sisters-in-law as well as sisters, and Brand and Brett would be brothers-in-law as well as brothers."

"My sister the idealist." Kim chuckled. "Brett would also have to fall in love with me. That's the problem with that plan."

"He asked you riding—that's a good indication he's on his way."

"That's ridiculous. I barely know him. Besides, I have my job to consider. I don't have time to fall in love."

Josie shook her head at her sister. "*I've* got a

job. *I'm* also in love. I'm not losing my job just because I'm marrying Brand."

Kim played with the strap of her purse. "You mean, you're going to continue working?"

"Sure, for a while. Maybe until I get pregnant."

"Brand's cool with that?"

"Of course. Besides, Tyler will have to find someone else to work for him if I don't continue. Later, though, I might even go back and get the rest of my law degree."

Kim smiled. "Josie, I thought you were going to live under Brand's thumb."

"No way. Me?" She pointed at herself with the key. "But I want love as well, Kim. So I'll love Brand and look after him."

"I'm not sure I could work and be really committed to a man."

"Maybe you're not cut out to be married, Kim. I am. And so is Brand. Maybe Brett isn't either, but I think he's looking. Brand says he's been restless since we announced our engagement, so Brand figures he's thinking it might be nice to tie the knot himself."

"It seems to me that everyone who gets married thinks everyone else should be married. And then when they get divorced, they think everyone else should get divorced. Anyway, I don't even live here. It makes no sense to even pair me up with Brett." She climbed out of the car and slammed the door.

"You could move back here," Josie said as they rang the doorbell.

"I don't want to," Kim said, even if she couldn't get the ride this morning out of her head. To ride over Stanton Farm each morning would be sheer heaven. And Brett knew she felt that way. That was the trouble. He knew exactly what she was going through. They were alike. Josie wasn't wrong.

The dressmaker was a thirty-five-year-old woman with long blond hair, which she wore in a pony tail. Her name was Isobel, and she had two small children, another on the way, and a husband who worked at Churchill Downs. How she managed to design beautiful dresses in the frantic, disorganized atmosphere she lived in, Kim didn't ask, but she was impressed. Josie's dress was a froth of white lace over satin. Her own dress was also made of satin, in a color called lemon mist. It was a design that flowed gracefully over Kim's tall frame. She felt very sophisticated in it.

Josie danced around in front of her as she stood for her fitting. "It looks wonderful on you, Kimmy. I'm so pleased. We chose the material to go with your hair and crossed everything that it would work out."

Isobel laughed and stuck some pins into a tuck. "I'm relieved as well. When Josie said, copper hair, I immediately thought green, but then, isn't green overdone on redheads."

"Even though I wear it quite a bit," Kim acknowledged and looked at herself in the mirror. She did appear quite elegant. She would definitely keep her big-city image in this dress. "It's beautiful. I can't believe you designed this from seeing my photograph, Isobel."

"That's how I work. You know, if you really don't like it, say something. I'll change the design."

"No, I love it," Kim said.

"We're having shoes done to match," Josie said. "You have to choose a pair in your size. Isobel has some here."

Once everything was chosen and sized, Josie seemed relieved. They went for coffee afterward in the little cafe attached to the bookstore owned by Kim's friend Gina.

Gina served three cups of coffee, then sat down with Kim and Josie. Gina was Kim's age, with curly black hair and big brown eyes, which she turned in Kim's direction. "So what do you think of your little sister snagging one of the richest men in town?"

"Unbelievable," Kim said, not letting any of her prejudice show. She was going to make a concerted effort to hide all that from now on.

Josie leaned over and patted Gina's tummy. "And what do you think of your friend, Kim, having a baby, at last."

Kim looked at Gina. "No way?"

"Absolutely."

"Is Tom thrilled?"

"Over the moon," Gina said.

"Are you still going to keep the bookstore going?"

"Naturally. I only live upstairs."

Kim glanced from Gina to Josie. "Well, you two seem to be able to combine work, love, and marriage."

"Don't you think you could?" Gina asked.

"I don't think so. None of my friends in Chicago can."

"It's different here in Valleyview. It's a slower way of life."

"You've said it." Josie said. "But I wouldn't give it up. I like it here."

Kim did too, really, but she wasn't going to admit it.

Kim was able to relax a little that evening. Josie went out with Brand. Her mother and father settled in front of the television, and Kim joined them. During a commercial she prepared a bowl of popcorn and passed it around. Her parents rarely spoke to one another, and she figured if this was all there was to marriage, no wonder she didn't really aspire to it.

Even so, once she was in bed, she kept thinking of the horse ride this morning with Brett. She wanted more. Then she wondered if it was really more riding she wanted, or more of Brett she wanted. She didn't want to answer that thought, but she knew the answer was, more of Brett. She was falling in love with him, just like that. Or had she always been attracted to him? Was that half her trouble? Did she pit the Stanton family against the Russell family because she was continuously fighting a pull toward Brett? No way, she told herself. She had hardly known him in those days. He had been barely out of his teens himself. He hadn't been the man he was today. And the man he was today was the man who attracted her. Fiercely attracted her.

Kim sat up in bed and held her head in her hands. *Keep rational, Kim. You're here, there's a wedding. It's nothing to do with Brett, or how you feel, it's all to do with Josie and Brand. Make it Josie and Brand's time. Forget yourself and all your own hangups. Everything will be fine once you return to Chicago and the promotion. Just think how great it will to take over Rosemary's office. You'll be able to replace all her family photos with photos of your own family. You'll be a boss, Kim. That's your goal. It has always been your goal. Don't do anything foolish, Kim.*

Far too wound up to sleep, she climbed out of bed. With her arms resting on the windowsill she looked out over the town. The moon hung low and bright in the sky, and it soothed her to look at it, to know that the expanse of nature and the universe was far beyond her small predicament. She would be fine. She would shroud herself among her family members. She would give everything of these next few days to Josie, and she would ignore Brett.

Chapter Four

In the morning, Kim's father went on his rounds to various farms. Josie went in to work for her last day before her wedding, and Moira went to her part-time job at the supermarket. Left alone in the house, Kim familiarized herself with everything—ornaments she recalled from her childhood and photographs of the family. When there was a loud knock on the door around eleven thirty, she went to answer it, thinking it might be a customer for her father.

It was Brett, wearing dark slacks, a white shirt, black tie, and his black leather jacket.

With one hand resting against the doorpost, he eyed her jeans and sweatshirt. "Didn't you remember lunch?"

Kim's fingers clutched the edge of the door. "You didn't confirm it."

His eyes twinkled. "I thought you would remember."

"I didn't think that you wanted to go to lunch because you didn't mention it again." And that was the truth.

He gave a shrug, and she thought she saw his eyes cloud a little, but he looked at his watch to hide any discomfort. "I have an hour and a half to spare and I was going to take you along to a new restaurant that serves the type of food to put some meat on your hips so you'll fit your old jeans once more. Therefore, can I come in while you change clothes?"

Kim let out a sigh. "I don't want to put on weight, Brett. We really don't have to go for lunch. I don't feel like it."

"I promised I would take you for lunch, Kim. Let me in."

She let him in and closed the door.

He turned to look at her. "Go get changed into some nice slacks or something."

Annoyed with him for being so bossy, she exhaled a sharp breath. "Brett. Stop acting as if you want to control me. I'm not your girlfriend. And I don't have to dress up like a Stanton just because my sister is marrying one."

He stared at her, shaking his head back and forth. "Why are you being like this?"

"Because I don't think we need to be together before the wedding, Brett."

He eased back on the heels of his casual black shoes. "I think we do. Especially if you're going to behave like this. We obviously have some issues to settle."

"We don't have any issues, that's the point, Brett. We never have had issues. Okay, we share a secret, but as you've already pointed out, it's not a secret that has anything to do with Josie or Brand, so it'll remain a secret. Anything else . . . well, there isn't anything else."

"Sorry to disappoint you, but there is."

"I don't know what you mean."

"You'll find out. Now go get ready. I'm starved."

She didn't want to go out with him. She knew what was happening to her. She had known last night in bed. She felt as if she were poised at the edge of a huge canyon, ready to plummet.

"Kim," he urged, pointing to his expensive gold watch.

It's only for a few days, not even the entire week, she told herself as she walked upstairs. People don't fall in love that fast anyway. Love takes time to develop. Doesn't it?

Kim put on her black slacks with a white cotton sweater. She brushed her hair, added some makeup, and a little lipstick. She didn't feel she needed a coat. Brett was holding a framed photograph of her when she came back to the living room.

"This is you when you were sixteen," he said, showing her the photograph.

She was surprised he could pinpoint her age so accurately. She didn't particularly like how she looked in that time period. Her hair had frizzy ends and was uncontrollable when she was younger. She had also been plumper. Now she went for expert hair trims and blow-drys at an exclusive beauty parlor, and kept her slim shape by watching her diet and playing indoor tennis on the weekend with some friends.

She curled her lip at the photograph. "I'm full of baby fat in that."

Brett gazed solemnly at the picture. "I don't think so. I think you look healthy and full of fun. You have a glimmer in your eyes that you don't have anymore. You're more guarded now." He cleared his throat and placed the frame back on the top of the sideboard. He glanced at her. "Ready?"

Kim tucked the long strap of her small black purse over her shoulder and met his eyes. Who was guarded? Brett's eyes seemed to have become enigmatic and cool. "Yes, I'm ready."

Kim had never walked in Valleyview with a Stanton beside her before, and she was aware of one or two stares from car windows. Or was she imagining the stares? Did anyone care anymore who went with whom? And why should she?

The restaurant was attached to the Bed and Breakfast Inn. It was in the back and overlooked a flower garden and a goldfish pond. The owners were new in town, and no one there seemed to know her. The menu was varied. She could have eaten a salad with oranges and raspberry dressing, but she realized she was hungry and went for the clam chowder and homemade bread, the same as Brett.

"It is delicious," she told Brett as they ate.

"I'd like to bring you here for the evening meal."

Kim stopped eating. "You don't have to go that far."

"Now what do you mean by that?"

"You don't have to entertain me endlessly just because I'm Josie's sister."

He finished chewing some bread. "What if I want to entertain you endlessly?"

She met his gaze. "It depends on whether I want to be entertained endlessly or not."

"Well, do you?"

Did she? She couldn't answer that, so she fumbled with her spoon and finished her soup.

He grinned. "I didn't hear your answer."

"I didn't give an answer, that's why."

"Why not?"

"*Brett.* I came here for a wedding, not for . . ."

"A fling?"

"You could say that," she agreed. "I'm going home next Tuesday. I'm barely here."

"Now you see her. Now you don't."

Kim chuckled.

"We'll come here for dinner on Monday evening then. Our last date."

"This is a date?"

"What else would you call it?"

He looked innocent, and Kim didn't trust him. Was he doing this because he was truly attracted to her, as Josie suspected, or was it merely to amuse himself because he was restless, as Brand had pointed out?

"Well, what do you call it when a man and a woman have lunch together?"

"I have lunch with men for business reasons."

"Ah, of course, you're tuned into city living. Well, then, let's say this is business. I'm headhunting you for a job." He glanced at his watch. "I have a business appointment in twenty minutes. Do you want to accompany me to my appointment? Then you can actually say this wasn't a date in your city language."

Kim began to laugh. "Brett. It's not a date. We had lunch because we're going to be family. That's all. And I don't want a job. I've told you that already."

"Okay," he said. "But the offer is still open. Come with me anyway. It's just a quick visit somewhere."

"All right," she agreed. She didn't have any-thing else to do but mooch around the house, and she was curious as to what type of job he was offering her. "I mean, I might know someone who does want a job in Valleyview, and then I would know more about it."

"Exactly."

Brett glanced around for a waiter and asked for the check. After the payment was dealt with, they walked back to the house and took off in a black Mercedes with a Stanton *S* license plate. Kim pushed aside the tiny little buzz of pleasure she felt as she sat inside the car next to Brett. What more could she want on a Wednesday afternoon than a handsome man in a fantastic car? If she forgot about everything but the immediate pres-ent, she could make herself feel as if she were on top of the world. She just didn't want to climb to the top of the world with Brett and then get pushed off and injured. She'd always been that way. She'd never wanted to get close to her dates. She liked her heart to stay intact. It was the only way she could control her mind.

"What are you thinking?" he asked as they drove through the lush countryside.

"What are you thinking?" she retorted.

He grinned. "That I like having you beside me."

She wished he wouldn't flirt. It made it so much more difficult to remain aloof.

They went to a house situated in a placid valley. The sign outside mentioned it was a graphics and printing company. Inside, Brett introduced her to a man named Mike Colvin. They had a few items to discuss, items that Kim listened to because the work was so closely related to her own. Yes. She could handle this. Stanton Farm ran advertisements in magazines, printed up brochures, and Brett even published articles about new procedures with horses and breeding. It would be fascinating work. She was far more attuned to horses than perfumes and soap.

"It seems very interesting," she said on the trip back to Valleyview.

He glanced at her with a smile. "You want the job then?"

"No. I wasn't saying that exactly."

"But you'll consider it?"

"No. Because I don't want to move back to Valleyview. However, I will definitely ask around my friends and see if anyone is interested. Everyone I know is an artist of some type."

He wasn't smiling anymore. "They have to know horses."

"I realize that."

"That's why I thought of you. You would be your own boss. I want to hand the responsibility to someone capable."

She was delighted that he thought her capable, but she couldn't imagine living back in Valleyview and working with Brett.

He dropped her off at home and took off. Kim let herself back into the silent house. She walked straight into the living room and touched the frame with her photograph that Brett had touched. Her fingers trembled against the gilt edging. It was like touching him.

She heard the front door open and her fingers came away from the frame as if they had been burned. It was her mother.

"Hi, Kim. Did you just stay around the house all day?"

She didn't think she should tell her mother she had been on what Brett had termed a date with him, or complicate matters by mentioning the job offer, so she shrugged. "I didn't go out far."

"Oh, well, I suppose you could do with a rest. We're eating out this evening. Josie came into the supermarket at lunch to tell me she had booked at Marseilles. It's a little French restaurant. It's her treat."

"Sounds good," Kim said, and went upstairs to shower and get ready for the outing: another restaurant meal. At this rate, she would definitely put on the weight Brett seemed to think she needed to gain.

Kim had a pleasant family evening. She was pleased. Without the Stantons there, her mother was relaxed and her father was more witty than usual. Josie made sure she treated them all to a delectable meal.

"This is all a bribe," she told Kim on the way home in the car. "I want you to come with me tomorrow to finalize some arrangements."

"Sure. That sounds like fun," Kim said.

The next day Kim thought she was going alone with Josie to make the arrangements for the rings, the flowers, and the caterers, so when Brand and Brett arrived to go with them, she was obviously shocked. She didn't want to be with Brett again.

Both men came into the house, right into the kitchen. Brand kissed his fiancé, while Kim stood around feeling awkward. She didn't glance at Brett. Didn't he have more work to do?

"I wish you would get your nose out of the air," Brett said, while Josie and Brand were still nuzzling one another.

Kim met his green gaze, which for her was rather like looking out over Kentucky Bluegrass fields—unsettling and beautiful. She shook her head to stop such capricious thoughts. "I don't know why you are here. Again."

"To buy stuff."

"What stuff?"

"I thought you and I should escape to purchase the happy couple a gift."

"I already purchased dishes and cutlery in Chicago before I left and had them shipped to the farm from the department store."

"Well, I don't have anything substantial. I'm giving them a check, but I want to also give them a gift for their new home."

"Which isn't built yet."

"It will be."

"You don't need me to help choose, Brett."

"Yes, I do. You're your sister's sister."

Kim narrowed her eyes at him. "Brilliant deduction."

Brent chuckled. "Cheer up. We don't do badly

together. We had a good ride the other morning, and yesterday was fun."

"I suppose," she admitted.

Brett laughed. "Hey, you two," he said to Brand and Josie. "Come on. Let's go. Otherwise Kim and I are going to feel like third and fourth wheels."

Josie and Brand climbed in the back seat of Brett's vehicle. Kim got in the front and fastened her seatbelt.

"This is great," Josie said. "I have this vision of us being a foursome."

Kim clenched her teeth together. How many more days did she have to endure with this pull toward Brett inside her? She would read her promotion material this evening, and she would call John right away tomorrow and accept the position. She wanted something firm to pull her back to Chicago.

She heard Brett chuckle. "Don't count on it, Josie. Your sister is a high flyer."

"And you're not I suppose," Kim retorted. "Cut it out, Brett. You're at the top of your ladder. You were born there. You had no rungs to climb. I've had to climb and crawl and scrape up every step. It's difficult."

Kim heard Josie gasp at her tirade, and Kim glared out the window, finding that the bright warm sunshine today taunted her mood. Now she had wrecked her sister's wedding. Darn. What was wrong with her? Didn't she like keeping a secret that burned in her stomach like acid? Or was it that she was being forced into the company of a man who even knew the reason for that secret? Or didn't she like this attraction he tugged out of her soul? Why hadn't Frank Stanton just put his leather-booted foot firmly onto the soil and vetoed the liaison? Or was it that Kim didn't know the first thing about love, and the pull of love? And maybe Frank Stanton did understand.

She glanced at Brett, her eyes taking in his profile, his broad shoulders, the strength of his wrists, the blunt-nailed fingers clasping the steering wheel. What would happen to her if she did fall in love with Brett? He wouldn't love her. She couldn't see in a million years that she would be the woman to finally light his fire.

Their first stop was the caterers, which was not far out of Valleyview. Kim and Brett didn't go into the small white building with the other two.

Brett said sternly, after a silence. "I'm not going to wreck their wedding. Why are you?"

Kim lowered her head and stared at her entwined hands. "What I said was the truth."

"Maybe in your mind it was. But I've had to work hard as well. Dad expected manual labor from the time I was a small kid. I've dragged my butt out of bed so many times against my will, it's been misery. And then it was Harvard. You're expected to pass at Harvard."

Kim glanced at him. "Didn't you?"

"Yes. But only because I put my nose to the grindstone. I'm not like Brand. Brand's naturally bright. He floats through everything. Yet my father expected the miracles from me."

"Probably because he passed the bulk of the business to you."

"Possibly. And I intend to make a success of it."

"It's already a success, Brett."

"Maybe on the circumference, but there have been some lean times. The economy isn't always booming. A few years ago a lot of the farms around Valleyview were sporting 'For Sale' signs."

"But not Stanton Farm."

"Only because we persevered and held on."

Kim rubbed her forehead. "Don't give me sob stories, Brett. Please. Because I can give you some back." She plunked her head against the headrest and stared out of the windshield.

Brett leaned over her. He said softly, "Poor little thing. Poverty-stricken, Kim." Then he kissed her.

His mouth was hard and determined on hers, the pressure of his lips creating a sudden warmth inside her. But she held herself still and unyielding, even if she wanted to wrap her arms around him and give in. When he drew back from her, looking at her with heat in his eyes, she swallowed hard, but she couldn't help her eyes from being locked with his.

He stroked her cheek with his knuckle. "Love-starved as well, aren't you?"

"No."

"Yes, you are. You need a relationship like Josie's to brighten your hazel eyes and make you loosen up."

"No. I don't, Brett. I'm not like Josie. Don't listen to what she says. She's always been more of a dreamer. I'm a practical person."

"I'm practical as well, but I would loosen up for love."

"Love? What are we talking about love for, Brett? Don't tell me such trash."

He grinned. "Ah, now you sound like a Valleyview gal."

"I do not."

"Oh, yes you do. Because you are."

He kissed her lightly on the mouth again, and this time Kim couldn't help her mouth softening a little beneath his. Then she realized that was giving in to him, and she tightened her lips until he withdrew.

"Before this weekend is over," Brett said, his breathing slightly ragged, "I want you to put your arms around me and kiss me like you mean it."

Kim wanted to do that right this moment, but she wouldn't give him the satisfaction of breaking her down. She wouldn't break down herself. She didn't know why he was doing this. Some perverse amusement, she supposed. She shook her head hard. "No way, Brett. I've got a big promotion at work. I'm going back to Chicago. I'm not staying in this . . . place." She rubbed her fingers across her mouth, but she didn't erase Brett's kiss. It thrummed through her like some ancient rhythm, as if he'd left the radio on low.

She heard him let out a long strangled breath, and she wanted to jump from the vehicle and run. But at that moment the other two came out of the building.

The florist was another small store, and, to Kim's relief, this time they all went inside. The scented, watery-floral aroma was appealing, and Kim lost herself among the attractive bouquets, trying to make herself feel more normal. But she couldn't forget Brett's kiss, or his words. Was he toying with her? What was he doing with her? Why was he doing it? Just to amuse himself because he had to go through this charade of being family with her?

"Kim," Josie called out. "Come over here and look at the arrangements."

Kim went to the counter where the others were. Brett leaned in his insolent manner against the counter. Brand shared Josie's enthusiasm for the arrangements in the big book.

"I want everything perfect," Josie said, stroking a photograph of lemon and mauve daisies. "Do you like those?"

"Well," Kim said, thinking about the Stanton image. "What else is there?"

Kim stopped her sister from flipping more pages. "I think the sweetheart roses. They're lovely."

Brett nudged his arm against hers. "I like the roses," he said.

Brand laughed. "They'll look sweet on you, Brett." Brand massaged Josie's shoulders affectionately. "I like the roses as well, darling. We'll have tons of roses."

The next stop was an elegant shopping mall. Here they split up. Josie and Brand were going to pick up their rings and a few other items. Brett wanted to buy his special gift. They decided to meet for coffee in two hours by the food court, where they would make the decision what to do next.

Kim found herself browsing gift stores with Brett. He took hold of her hand.

"You feel cold," he said.

"You don't help."

"Cut it out, Kim." He stopped in front of a store that had expensive gifts and pretended to stare into the window at the goods. "Tell me about this promotion."

Everyone was right: Brett did have one of those minds that stayed fixated with a subject until he'd exhausted it. "I've been an Assistant Art Director for three years, and I've been offered the position of the Art Director, because she's leaving."

He bent his head sideways to try and read a price tag on one of the goods. "That's what you want?"

"Of course. It will be more money, more prestige. Longer hours, naturally, but it's what I'm working toward."

His fingers squeezed hers. "Your ultimate goal, in other words."

His touch made her head spin. "Not my ultimate goal," she said shakily. "There are higher positions. There's Creative Director, and then there's partner."

He glanced at her. "And that's what you eventually want to work up to?"

"Yes," she said.

"You're doing that clawing and climbing thing you say you do, all the time then?"

"Yes. That's how it is in my company. Everyone is out for themselves."

"And you like that?"

"I'm a goal-oriented type of person, Brett. I have to be that way."

"Why?"

"Because I haven't had everything handed to me on a silver platter the way you have," she whispered harshly. "Don't undermine me."

He drew her nearer to him. "You know what I want?"

Kim shook her head.

"I want that sixteen-year-old back again."

"Why?"

"Because you were a real person then. Now you're a robot of the greed generation."

"Oh, come on, Brett. You can't say that of me. You, who runs one of the biggest breeding enterprises for racehorses in Kentucky. That's hypocrisy."

"No. My grandfather made Stanton Farms famous. My father continued the operation. I'm bringing it into the twenty-first century. That's all. And I love what I do. I love the animals. I love it. That's the difference between us, Kim."

"I love my job," she said, but her words sounded as hollow as she sometimes felt inside. Sometimes she loved her job, but other times she was bored out of her mind, trapped inside a high-rise office block, with the city culture pressing around her. Her promotion would change all that though. When she had Rosemary's salary, she could move to a larger apartment, at a more prestigious location. She could shop at the better stores and wear clothes that would never be looked down on by the Stanton family. Not that anyone had actually looked down on her since she had been here. But she felt that way inside, and one day—she had promised herself a long time ago—she wouldn't feel that way inside ever again.

"Therefore you won't consider my job offer at all?"

"I told you I didn't want to move back to Valleyview."

"Or don't you want to work for a Stanton? Is that it? You think you would be following in your mother's footsteps."

"That's not it, Brett. I've got a perfectly good job with great prospects, and I don't want another one. All right?"

Brett let her go of her hand abruptly. "Let's go and get this gift."

Well, she didn't want his attention. She didn't have it. Brett moved through the rest of his choice stores in a businesslike manner. Eventually, he chose a painting of Valleyview by a renowned local area artist. He asked for it to be delivered to the farm on Friday.

Yes, Mr. Stanton.

Thank you, Mr. Stanton.

Kim heard those words from the store clerk and made a note to remember them. Whatever Brett said about his climb, about his difficulties, about proving himself, he was still a Stanton. Just the name held clout. *Remember that Kim. You have worked for everything you have. Don't let him take it away from you by admitting there are doubts and hollow areas of your life. Pretend it's the greatest thing on earth. Whatever he says, if you worked for him, he would be the boss.*

Kim thought the day might end after coffee in the food court. However, Josie and Brand wanted to go and to see a blues band at a club on the outskirts of Lexington.

"The food is great there," Josie said. "We'll have a cool time."

Kim didn't want a cool time. She only wanted to get home and read about her promotion, so she could accept it. Her attraction to Brett was like being on the end of a rope for tug-of-war, and knowing it might throw her to the losing side at any moment.

However, she did have quite a cool time. The food was delicious, and by the time it was served, Kim was hungry for the succulent chicken, green salad, and a baked potato, which, for once, she covered with sour cream. The basic blues roots music was also entertaining. It was obvious Josie and Brand had been here often together. They seemed to be a cohesive couple, with similar tastes and senses of humor. As they sat side by side, Brand always had his arm around Josie, and he was often caressing and stroking her back or shoulder. Kim felt quite left out. Brett was acting as if he'd had ice water injected into his veins, which was probably her own fault. She had turned down his job offer. She had fought with him. And really all he was doing, as far as she knew, was being polite and including her in the wedding preparations. They could have left her at home. She didn't have to be here with them. Really she wasn't being very nice to Josie.

Kim decided that this situation wouldn't do. She must think more positively about the wedding. She had to forget the past and at least make it seem that she and Brett were friends. Surely she could treat Brett as a flirtation. It might be fun for the wedding. It didn't mean to say she had to be serious with him. Why did she always think so seriously? Other women went out and had good times. Josie and Brand were dancing, having a great time. She glanced over the table at Brett and smiled at him.

Brett's lip curled. "Now what's up?"

"I've decided I'm going to do as you suggest and enjoy myself this weekend."

"Well, I'm pleased you've made that decision. I don't like miserable dates."

"I'm not your date, Brett. We've settled that already."

"You are my date. So let's dance and let the other two see we're cool with one another. Why cause stress?"

He stood up and lifted her hand so she was forced to rise to her feet as well. He had taken off his leather jacket, so he only wore a lightweight blue cotton shirt and tie. He led her to the small round dance floor and she slipped into his arms. Kim had to place her hand on his waist by his belt and her other hand on his shoulder. His muscles flexed beneath her fingers and she felt him stroke her hair down her back.

"I like your hair like this."

"Josie keeps insisting on crimping it."

She felt him swallow a breath. "She knows what looks good on you." His arms tightened around her.

Knowing definitely she was falling for him now, Kim allowed herself to close her eyes and listen to the husky voice of the male singer on the record. *Why Brett out of all the men she had met and dated?*

The music flowed around them as they danced. Brett didn't say anything else until Brand and Josie danced up beside them.

"We're getting tired," Brand said. "Do you want to call it a night?"

Brett glanced at Kim. "Yes, I think so. I have an early morning meeting. I don't know how you two keep going."

"We're in love," Josie told him. "And I can't sleep anyway. I'm getting married on Saturday."

"Oh, I almost forgot," Brett teased her as they all walked back to their table to collect their belongings.

Josie whispered as they walked out of the club, "You two are falling in love with one another. I can just tell."

"No we're not, Josie," Kim protested.

Brett was silent all the way home. Kim watched the dark countryside pass outside the window. In the back seat, Josie and Brand cuddled up. Leaving the other two in the vehicle, Brett walked Kim to the porch.

"Tomorrow evening the gifts are being displayed in their apartment at the house. So I'll come and get you."

"Can't I just come alone?"

"How are you going to get there?"

"With my parents."

"No you are not. Your parents will be there earlier with Josie. They are going to help with setting up the gifts."

Kim made a comical face. "Oh, why didn't someone give me a schedule so I would know these things?"

"You knew it would be a busy time, Kim. You said you were going to lighten up. So, do so. See you tomorrow."

He ran down the steps and let Josie out of the four-wheel-drive. He gave her a kiss on her cheek, and her sister joined Kim. They went into the house.

"Do you want to stay up and chat?" Josie asked.

Kim ran her fingers through her hair. "I'm really tired. Aren't you?"

"No, I'm wound up like a top. I'm so excited." Josie grinned. "I'm going to have hot milk. Come on, Kimmy. Like old times."

Kim succumbed to Josie's cups of hot milk heated in the microwave. Josie stirred chocolate powder into hers.

"Why can't you get along with Brett?"

Kim sipped her drink. "I suppose I don't think I would have a chance with him."

"Do you want a chance?"

"Don't you say a word to him, Josephine Russell."

Josie stirred in more chocolate and drank some. "Great. A chocolate fix. Oh, I won't say a thing. But Brand thought you would make a good couple. He thinks Brett should settle down."

"Does he run around with a lot of women then?"

"No. He's like you: work work work. But he's been quite a cool dude since you've come home, so . . ." Josie shrugged. "You never know you might be the one."

To light his fire, Kim added, as she went upstairs, carrying the rest of her hot milk. No, she didn't think so. She didn't think so at all. Whatever Brett said, he needed by his side someone like Tessa O'Brien, a tall willowy blonde with social breeding. Not a scrappy career woman who had clawed her way halfway up the promotion ladder and intended to get right to the top.

Kim wasn't really tired. She was wound up as well, but for different reasons than Josie. She undressed, put on a robe, and sat at the tiny desk in her childhood bedroom and began to read about the promotion. Partway through she knew she had been conned. This was a promotion of sorts, but she was to share Rosemary's full position with a man, which immediately meant less money. More than she was getting now, but less than Rosemary. And what would it make her? Another assistant. She knew how the women were treated at C&C. If you didn't make noises, you were a doormat.

Disappointed, Kim rose from her chair, fighting ragged emotion. She wondered, if she didn't accept the promotion, would it mean the end of her job? She had known employees who hadn't accepted promotions, and sank back into their former positions. Eventually they were shoved out of the company, or left because the effort wasn't worth it anymore if there was nowhere higher to go.

So, she supposed she would have to accept, even if it wasn't what she had planned. She would fight the man she would share the position with, so she wouldn't be a doormat. She would survive. But once in bed, she felt the disappointment and despair wash right through her entire body. Chicago and her job were her escape from Valleyview. C&C had just loosened the latch on her escape hatch and made it less secure.

Chapter Five

Kim knew she should phone John first thing in the morning to accept the promotion, but she couldn't make herself pick up the phone and dial the number of her office. She stuffed the envelope into the bottom of her bag. Why did it have to be a share position? Why couldn't it have been a real honest-to-goodness promotion?

She paced around her bedroom, thinking that what she really needed right now was a gallop over the fields of Stanton Farm to clear her mind. Except she didn't want to ask her mother if she could borrow her car for that reason, when she knew her mother wasn't keen about her seeing Brett. Right now everything was moving smoothly toward the wedding, so she didn't want to make any waves. And she was also going for lunch with Josie to meet Deanna, Brett's sister, at Fishburn Farms, so there wasn't time to ride anyway. She supposed she had better use her energy to sort out something to wear for the lunch.

"Something the matter?" her mother asked her when Kim came downstairs, ready for the lunch, dressed in her black suit with a white lace blouse, her hair in a tightly coiled bun.

"No. Why?"

"You don't look as if you're relaxing at all."

"A wedding isn't exactly relaxing, Mother, especially a wedding to a Stanton." Although yesterday, hadn't she made a pledge to enjoy herself? And wasn't she the one who thought she shouldn't make waves?

Moira made a face. "I wish you hadn't been with me that evening, Kim. I really do. Then you wouldn't have to shoulder the burden."

"At least you've had me to share it with, Mom. Although, I would like to know what it was all about."

Her mother rubbed her neck. "Please, Kim. It's quite embarrassing for me."

"What did you do?" Kim asked.

"I almost . . . stress, the almost, sweetie. There was a flirtation between me and Frank Stanton."

Kim hadn't expected that, although she wasn't

quite sure what she had expected. "What do you mean, 'almost'?"

Moira slumped into a kitchen chair. "How old was I then? In my early forties. Your father has never, well never really been a loving man. Although, I do know he loves me. He's just not . . . demonstrative."

Kim supposed she did know that. Her parents weren't ones for kissing and hugging. "So you and Frank Stanton . . ."

"No." Moira cut her off. "I didn't go through with it. There were a few stolen kisses here and there. He would surprise me in different rooms. It was exciting for a while. But he wanted more, and I chickened out, I suppose. That night I told him no. He didn't accept it. He went ballistic. He told me . . . oh dear. He told me he was in love with me."

Kim slumped in an opposite chair. This was far from what she had expected. "Were you in love with him?"

Moira appeared to be gasping for air. "It would have been easy, but I didn't let myself. The yelling that night wasn't because he dismissed me. I gave him my notice and told him I wouldn't be back, and he tried to stop me."

"Mom, what's it like now with him?"

"Strained, but we're getting through it. We

haven't mentioned anything. I stuck by your father, Kim."

"I don't know how you can face Frank."

"I do what I have to. And that's all there is to it. Now I want you to forget what I've told you, and don't say a word to anyone."

"I think Brett might know."

Moira nodded. "He does. One day he came home when I was there in the afternoon, and his father had his arm around my waist. I knew he figured it out."

"What about Liz?"

"I don't think she knows. She doesn't act as if she does. She lives in a rather funny world anyway. She's very vague. I think Frank was reacting to her indifference, or whatever it is. Anyway, the flirtation is long over. It's finished. It's nothing to do with now."

Kim shook her head. "You must have been devastated when Josie began dating Brand."

Moira half-smiled. "I was floored. I couldn't believe it. I hoped it would be merely a flash-in-the-pan type of thing, but it began to get serious and I knew I was going to have to face the past."

"You should have told me years ago, Mom."

"No, you wouldn't have understood then. I don't know if you really understand now."

Kim thought of Brett and the pull he had for

her. "I think I do now," she said softly. "I think I do."

Moira patted her fingers. "I've always counted on you, Kim. You're strong."

"You know what I thought it was all this time?"

"What?"

"I thought it was because you were a sloppy housekeeper. Remember you burned the dresser?"

Moira made a face. "Do I ever, but no one ever knew as far as I know. Liz smoked at that time as well."

"The other night, when we were there I went upstairs and saw that the dresser top had been refinished."

"Oh, Kim. It wasn't that. Frank never checked up on my housekeeping." Moira smiled slightly. "It wasn't really a bad reason to leave either. More heart-wrenching than anything. But I knew you always felt it was because of the class difference."

"You should have told me."

"No. You would have felt I had betrayed your dad. Now you know, I didn't. It's all over anyway, Kim. Let's forget it."

Stunned by her mother's confession, Kim went with Josie in her car to Deanna's farm, amazed that the men hadn't insinuated their way into the trip in some way, but pleased they hadn't. She didn't want to see Brett again for a while. He knew her mother had almost had an affair with his father. All this time he'd known. Had his flirtations with Kim been merely a reaction to that knowledge? Did he think her mother was an easy mark and that Kim would be the same—a little fling over the wedding weekend?

"Now what's wrong?" Josie asked as she drove through the Stanton gates.

Kim could hear by her sister's tone that Josie was beginning to get fed up with her. "Nothing," she said with a forced smile. It would catastrophic for Josie to know that story. It might not seem like much in the telling, but Kim herself knew the burden she had carried all those years. At least in some ways she'd been relieved of one burden. Frank hadn't dismissed her mother because of her lower class. Moira had left because Frank had been in love with her. Kim wondered if Frank had suffered over the departure. Or maybe he was the type of man who didn't suffer much. Maybe he tried to seduce all the housekeepers.

Josie parked the car. "Kim, I don't know what it is with you, but I can't stand your attitude much longer," Josie spoke in the same small determined voice she had used on Kim when she was a little girl and Kim had done something she didn't agree with. "Brett's a nice guy. Other women would be tickled to have him as their escort for the weekend."

Kim laid her hand on her sister's arm. "Josie, everything will be fine. We're just all tense."

"You more than everyone else," Josie retorted and ripped the keys from the ignition. "Even Brand mentioned he thought you were very standoffish to his family. We're all going to be even now. You don't have to worry about anything like Mom being their housekeeper anymore. She's going to be the mother of the bride."

Kim swallowed hard. Taken to task by her little sister, she thought. Her mother was handling this, so she could. She also had to do what she had to do. "Okay. I'll take the chip off my shoulder."

Josie laughed. "Please, would you." She reached out and tugged some ringlets down the side of Kim's cheeks. "You're not in the office now."

Deanna was older than her brothers. In her mid-thirties, she seemed extra thin and was more like her mother. Kim had never known the woman, so Josie introduced them. Then Deanna led them into a gracious living room that wasn't quite of the quality of Stanton Farm. But it reeked old money that the Russell family had never even hoped for. Kim told herself to stop thinking that way. Pretend you're equal, she told herself, as Deanna smiled at the two women.

"I'll have the lunch served. Stephanie will be home from school soon. She's on a half day today as she's finished now for the wedding. Brett was picking her up and going for a ride with her first."

Darn, Kim thought, that meant Brett would probably come into the house and she would have to see him again. Couldn't she be given a few hours peace from him? Each time she remembered his kiss, she scolded herself for being so silly and gullible. Is this how her mother had felt with Frank?

Deanna left and Josie said softly, "They've had some hard times."

"How?"

"They rely on race wins, and Gordon had a lot of lean years with some lousy horses and some terrible bad luck. One horse broke its leg in the middle of a race and had to be put down. It broke Gord up."

"It would break me up," Kim commented, placing her purse on the thick carpet beside the chair she sat in. She hated to think of a horse having to be put down prematurely. She hated to think about anything that had been daily news in Valleyview when she was young. She remembered crying for a week when a horse her father shod regularly had died. That kind of weakness she had put behind her when she went to college and stayed in Chicago to work. She was hardened to life's knocks now, which was why she really didn't need love.

"Anyway," Josie said, "they're just picking up now with some new horses they acquired from Brett. So hopefully things will be better. But all that strain caused marriage strife."

"Who told you this?" Kim said.

"They were going to get a divorce."

"Through Tyler?"

"Yep. But they called it off. Brand said they patched everything up. So hopefully, for Stephie's sake, they have. That's where Brett comes in. He's been really cool with Stephie. A super uncle to her, when her parents weren't really feeling up to having her around too much."

"You wouldn't think Brett was that type of man, would you?"

"What type of man?"

"To like children," Kim said impatiently. "But he did tell me he rode with Stephanie."

Josie smiled. "You try and hide how you feel about him, but I can see you're struck."

"I'm not, Josie. Please don't spread that around like a rumor. I'm only here until next week. Brett's not my type. I don't like those horsey type of men," Kim lied, and looked out of the window, over a farm that had as much great beauty as Stanton Farm. Everywhere around here was far too beautiful; there was far too much of a tug on her heart. She felt a moment of panic, that she had to leave now before she couldn't do so any longer.

Josie leaned back in her seat and crossed her long legs in cream silk pants. "What kind of men do you like now then, Kim?"

"Sophisticated men. City men."

Josie chuckled. "Surely you don't prefer wimps over hunks like Brett and Brand?"

"There are hunks in the city, Josie."

"I suppose." Her sister grinned. "Has Brett kissed you yet?"

His kiss wouldn't leave her. "Josie, please . . ."

"He has, hasn't he? I thought so. He kissed you yesterday, didn't he? Brand thought so."

"Do you discuss me with Brand all the time?"

"Not all the time." Josie fluttered her lashes. "We have other things we like doing, but we talk about a lot of stuff. Like he really wants to keep our marriage together. His parents had troubles at one time. Did you know that?"

Kim lowered her head and swallowed. "No. I didn't," she said airily, smoothing her pants before she raised her head again to look at her sister.

"Well, apparently they did, and Brand has made a definite commitment to me."

"He sounds like a really sincere man, Josie."

"I love him very deeply, Kim. I can't get out of this now."

Kim could tell. This wasn't a flash in the pan, as her mother had hoped. Moira had probably seen that and become resigned to the marriage. There was nothing anyone could do to break them up. Had Frank seen the same situation and also given his blessing in resignation?

Forget it, Kim, she told herself. *Just forget it all. It's eating you all up for nothing.*

Deanna returned with a maid, who served trays of appetizing sandwiches and finger food on the low tables interspersed between the chair arrangement.

Deanna sat down between them. "We can get started. Stephie will probably eat something with Brett after the ride. All girls together. We can have a chat. Aren't you just so excited, Josie?"

"My little heart is pitter-pattering all of the time," Josie said, picking up a slim salmon sandwich. She nibbled the food.

Deanna looked at Kim. "It's quite a thing, one

of my brothers getting married. I never thought they would."

"Why not?" Kim asked.

Deanna shrugged. "I don't know why not. I think because I still imagine them as small kids. I'm quite a bit older. I babysat them when they were little, especially Brand."

"Didn't you have a nanny?" Kim knew she shouldn't have asked such a pointed question, but Deanna had asked for it.

"Yes, we did, but Mother liked us to be close as a family."

"That's nice," Kim said in a more natural tone and added a smile. She reached for one of the sandwiches herself.

Deanna poured coffee from a silver pot.

"Brett likes Kim," Josie said.

Deanna kept her gaze on Kim. Kim could have strangled her sister. "Does he? Well, well. Maybe you Russell girls have something that we Stanton girls don't know about."

In that moment Kim knew that Deanna was the fifth person who knew of the thwarted affair between Moira and Frank. It was all over years ago, but Kim still worried that the more people who knew, the more chance there was of the gossip reaching Josie, or even Kim's father.

"What do we have that attracts the Stanton men, Kim?" Josie asked with a grin.

"Oh," Kim said. "Brett's just being polite because we're being paired up for the wedding. It's nothing really."

A cough by the door interrupted them, and Kim was extremely pleased to see Gordon Fishburn walk through. She knew him from her father's business. A forty-year-old man, not too tall, with broad shoulders and a complexion that showed he'd spent most of his working life outdoors. Kim thought he was handsome in a craggy way. She rose to shake Gordon's hand.

"Hi, Kim. Haven't seen you for years."

"I've been away for a while," she told him.

As she returned to her seat, Gordon teased Josie and kissed Deanna chastely on the cheek. As Gordon was eating lunch, Brett and Stephanie arrived. Kim loved Stephanie right away and could see why Brett enjoyed her company. With long black hair, a winning toothy smile, wearing jeans and a sweatshirt with a cat's face on the front, she was full of life and exuberance. She wanted to see Josie's ring again before she perched on the arm of Kim's chair and touched Kim's hair.

"Is it real?"

Her mother said, "Of course it's real. Isn't it, Kim?"

Kim had the impression Deanna wished it wasn't.

Brett moved into the conversation to save her. "I can vouch for it being real. I remember when she was younger. It was the same color."

"It's lovely. Like shimmery gold," Stephie said. "Brett told me you are a good rider, Kim. Are you going to come riding with us? We're going on Sunday, after the wedding and everything's over. We always go riding on Sundays, don't we, Uncle Brett?"

Brett nodded and rested his coffee cup and saucer on his knee. He raised an eyebrow at Kim. "Sure do. Kim will come. She's here for a few more days after the wedding, and she'll probably be at loose ends."

No, she wouldn't be at loose ends. She had her own friends to visit, and she wanted to spend more time with her parents.

"Cool," Stephie said. "Brett said you rode Princess, so you can have her again, Kim. I'll ride Smooth Flight. Uncle Brett just got her last year, and she's neat."

Kim wondered if she could beg off on Sunday by saying she was too tired after the wedding. Yes, that's what she would do, although she hated to disappoint the little girl.

Gordon didn't stay very long after he finished

eating. Brett left with him. Stephie grew tired of
the adult company and went to watch TV. The
maid disposed of the luncheon things, and Josie
decided to leave. When they were driving away,
Kim let out a breath of relief, but she didn't let
her sister see she was relieved. In fact, she started
up a conversation about some of their own friends
that had nothing to do with the Stantons and the
Fishburns.

But Josie was fixated on her new family-to-be.
"You will ride with Stephie on Sunday, won't
you, Kim? She doesn't like disappointments.
She's fragile because of all the family distress."

"I seem to be getting forced into being with
the Stantons."

"They're going to be family, that's why."

Kim realized that Josie wasn't stopping in
town.

"Where are we going now?" Kim asked.

"Out to see my building lot."

It wasn't going to change, ever now, Kim
thought as Josie drove into Stanton Farm and
along the road that she had taken with Brett the
morning they had ridden. Two men were looking
over a horse in the paddock near the main breeding station, and Josie called out to them through
the open window. Kim saw that one of the men
was Brett. He had obviously come home and put

on a blue check shirt, which he wore flapping outside his jeans. He waved. Josie went on and they climbed a small hill. She parked at the top, where a foundation had already been laid for a house.

Watching for muddy patches, Kim walked around the building site with her sister. When she looked across the property, there was a view ranging for miles, far beyond the Stanton acres. She could see the church spire in the valley.

"This is a fantastic view, Josie, isn't it?"

"It's great. We're having an extra story with a room upstairs so we can enjoy the view."

"What do you think?"

A male voice spoke behind them and Kim twisted around to see that Brett and Brand had walked up the hill to see them. Brand and Josie kissed and stood with their arms around one another's waists, looking with pride at their new home-to-be.

Brett hiked around the building lot as if making an inspection. Kim, who always felt a trifle awkward in the aura of Brand and Josie's love, followed him.

"It's coming along," he said. "They'll be in here by the end of the summer at this rate."

"That soon?" Kim asked, smoothing one of the escaping tendrils Josie had loosened earlier.

"Brand and Josie are paying for it themselves. They bought the land from Dad."

"You mean, they'll be like other people and have a mortgage?"

"A small one."

"Is this the Stanton way of teaching an heir how to manage money?" She thought Brett looked different in his cross-trainers, jeans, and casual shirt. More a man she felt in tune with. Her heart beat a little faster and her throat dried up.

"Oh, Kim," Brett said, and reached out to touch one of the bright tendrils of hair himself. "They wanted to do it that way. It was their choice. Dad still has a major stake in the farm. Brand and I draw a salary from the overall operation."

His touch sent shivers down her spine. "I thought you were in complete control."

He moved a step closer to her. "It's a business, Kim. We have staff. While Josie and Brand are busy with one another, come and see the office complex I told you about."

Brett shouted to the other couple that they would be back in a few minutes, and Kim walked with him down the hill to the large buildings clustered together. Some were the original brick buildings with white-painted trim, and others were new additions over the years that had attained the look of the old. The offices were part of the breeding complex, and Brett opened the door and stood aside to let her in. There were three offices and only one appeared to be occupied. On a table were two new computers not yet hooked up.

"I've moved into this building," Brett said, closing the door behind them. "I'm working on how to structure the organization. As I told you, I would really like someone for public relations and advertising."

Kim slipped her hands into the pockets of her black slacks. "Who does it now?"

"Me, or the manager, Ray Todd. While at one time it was merely a small piece of the action, it's been growing."

"There's no one in Valleyview you could hire?"

He shifted his hip on to a corner of a bare table. "Oh, possibly, but you came along with the qualifications, so I offered the position to you first."

She met his eyes. "I told you my decision."

He nodded. "I know. But I would really like you to reconsider, Kim."

"I have my promotion."

"Yes, and whatever you think, I'm not undermining that. It's just a thought, a chance for you to come home to a job involving horses and the things you love."

Kim swallowed. She would soon be including Brett in the things she loved. If she accepted his offer, she might end up working here and loving him from afar. She couldn't put herself into that vulnerable position, although this job would be more of a boss position than the one she had been offered by C&C. Why had Brett put her into this situation? Why couldn't he just do the wedding and leave it at that?

"Are you going to reconsider your original answer?" he asked.

"All right." What else could she say?

"No rush." He straightened. "Wait until after the wedding."

He led the way out the door and they walked up the hill again to where Josie and Brand were leaning against Josie's car, talking.

"What's going on?" Josie called out in a suggestive voice.

Kim glared at her sister. "Nothing. Brett was showing me some of the new premises."

"Neat, huh?" Brand said.

"Very neat," Kim agreed.

"Well, we're going now," Josie said, opening her car door. "Tonight it's the gift showing. See you later, honey."

Brett opened the passenger side door for Kim. She slid inside. He grinned at her. She half-smiled. He was so darn attractive.

"I'll pick you up later," he said.

She nodded.

The men waved as Josie drove back along the road and out of the Stanton Gates. Kim looked back at the farm. Once upon a time she had hoped never to visit here again. Now she felt as if she had left something behind her.

Chapter Six

Her parents left for the farm after dinner, and Kim went upstairs to look through her clothes. She hadn't brought enough with her, she decided, and began to fish around in her closet for something she had owned before she went to Chicago. She found a long black skirt splashed with orange and white flowers and a silk blouse in a paler orange to match. It was a color combination that should have clashed with her hair, but it never had. After a shower, she put the outfit on, not surprised to find the skirt and blouse rather loose on her. She had lost weight, lots of weight. As she stroked on makeup, she could see the structure of her cheekbones and fine lines beside her mouth. She knew it was because of the stressful competitive nature of her job and the life she lived now. It would probably do her good to slow down and live in Valleyview once again. What was she thinking about? Brett was making her doubt her lifestyle in the city. All she had to do when she got back was pace herself more evenly and watch her diet. Maybe take off the hour she was allowed to eat a nutritious lunch. Yes, that's all she needed to do to bring herself up to par again. She didn't need to move and change her job.

Kim had just slipped her feet into a pair of white sandals when she heard the doorbell ring. Brett. Running her hand down her hair to smooth it, she went downstairs to open the door. In the lamplight over the porch, Brett looked dark and mysterious in black slacks and shirt. Older than he had this afternoon in his jeans and check shirt. His eyes glittered like emeralds as he looked at her.

"Wow," he said, as she ushered him inside. "A little color gives you a vibrancy, doesn't it?"

She flicked the skirt with her fingers. "It's old."

His mouth narrowed. "You mean before you went away?"

She nodded. "Yes. That's what I mean. Now I'll just go get my purse. Do you want to wait here?"

"At the bottom of the stairs? Josie invites me into the kitchen when I come here."

Kim remembered the way the two brothers had walked casually into the kitchen the other day. "You mean, you've been here lots of times . . . before me?"

He smiled. "Before you? Not lots. I visited once since the marriage was planned."

"Why should the plans have to be made here?"

"Because Josie wanted to include your mother and father. Kim, don't question everything. There isn't another motive in this but love for Josie and Brand."

"I didn't think otherwise."

He placed his hand on the banister knob. "You act like this is a plot to overthrow you. It's not. That's all I'm saying."

"I'm just worried about the past, that's all. Your sister knows, doesn't she?"

"Deanna?"

"Isn't she your only sister?"

He smiled. "Yeah. No, I don't know who knows. I never said a word to anyone. If she does know, I'm not sure how she found out. She was already married to Gord by then. She wasn't living at home."

Kim shook her head. "Maybe I imagined it."

"I think you probably did." He checked his

watch. "Now, go on, get your purse. We don't want to be late."

Kim ran upstairs, aware of Brett below watching her. She slipped her black jacket over her arm, in case it grew cool later, and tucked her purse strap over her shoulder. She gazed once more at herself in the mirror. To loosen her nerves, she smiled widely. She kept the smile frozen all the way down to the bottom of the stairs.

Brett stood across the bottom, not allowing her access from the last step.

"Put your arms around my neck and kiss me, Kim."

She met his steady green gaze. "Why should I?"

His throat moved. "Because I want to kiss you before we go and we're surrounded by other people. One more step, honey, and you're close enough."

Kim could barely breathe as she moved one step down. She nearly toppled forward and put out her hand to save herself. Then she found her fingers clasping his black silk shirt, found her mouth devoured by his for a suspended moment.

Brett withdrew his mouth slowly, at the same time reaching down to capture her hand in his. He squeezed her fingers and she looked at him.

"It was good," he said softly. "But I'm still waiting for you to throw your arms around me."

"I would have to be in love with you to do that." She tried to insert humor into her tone.

"So the absence of love rules out all hugs, right?"

Kim shook her head. "Oh, I don't understand, Brett."

"No, you don't understand."

They left the house. Kim locked the door. When she reached his car, Brett held open the door and let her climb inside. Kim thought he banged the door too hard on her. Now what? Why couldn't they just be two people together, without all this tension? Even the trip to Stanton Farm remained tense and silent.

She looked at him once but he didn't look at her. He concentrated on his driving. She almost asked, what have I done? But she held her tongue. She didn't want to get any more involved with him. His kiss remained on her mouth, intense and indelible.

When they arrived at the farm, Brett helped Kim from the Mercedes and held her hand on the way to the front door. The door was open and Kim could hear a buzz of activity.

"Where is the guest suite?" she asked, hearing her voice sound shaky.

Brett cleared his throat. "Oh, it's through there." He pointed in the opposite direction to where he was leading her. "I want a cold drink first. Come on."

He led her into the sitting room they had been received in the other evening. It was silent. Brett let go of Kim's fingers and went over to a cocktail cabinet with a small refrigerator. He took out two cans of soda pop.

"Want one of these?" he asked.

"Please."

"Ice?"

"Please."

"So acquiescent," he said, plonking ice cubes into glasses.

He turned around with two full glasses and handed her one. He clinked the ice. "To us." He drank half the glass. "Do you ever want to fall in love and experience what Josie and Brand are experiencing?"

Why did he shoot off-the-shoulder questions at her like that? "I haven't considered it much until we've all started discussing it this past week," she said, sipping the cold soft drink. "Do you?"

"Yes, I think I would. I would like a kid like Stephie. A family life. I think Stanton Farm is made for a family. It's that type of place."

"That's no reason to get married."

"I'm not saying that's the reason, but I think I'm ready to settle down."

Brand had told Josie this. Now Brett had confirmed it. Kim felt something flutter in her throat. Her heart felt tight. "Then you will have to find that particular woman, who lights your fire."

"Yep, I will." He upended the glass and finished his drink. He placed it on a silver tray. "Have you finished yours?"

"Yes, thank you." Kim walked over to him and placed her glass on the tray next to his.

"Let's go then."

Kim walked with Brett along a corridor with floor to ceiling windows overlooking the property. It was a part of the house that hadn't been here ten years ago.

"Did you have this built on?" she asked, wanting to get onto more practical ground with him. He wanted a wife and family. And she wanted a career. That proved they were incompatible. But she could live here. She knew that. And he had offered a job that could bring her back here. She would be with her family again, and she would have a career. She could focus on that. If Brett eventually found the woman to light his fire then she would give him her blessings. He was showing her an entirely different man than she had ever thought he was. Actually, she was seeing a different side to Stanton Farm altogether. Everyone worked hard the same way as her family. That they had more family money was just part of life's bargain, she supposed. Her father could have built up his business earlier than his current success, but he'd never possessed the entrepreneurial skills necessary. Brett obviously had them.

"We had the extension built on for Brand and myself. My parents didn't like our loud music." He grinned.

She returned his grin. "Is that true?"

"Yes, it's true."

"You mean, your parents had an entire suite built on for their sons. Just like that."

"It wasn't just like that. As the business grew, we were entertaining more and more business acquaintances. Dad figured it would be a nice gesture to have a guest suite, which Brand and I could live in when we were home. Sometimes we liked to entertain our own friends away from the family."

"Girls?" Kim asked.

"Definitely girls," he teased.

"Have you dated lots of women, Brett?" Kim asked and heard her voice break as she spoke.

If he heard the break, he didn't make any indication. "Yes, I've dated my share," he said casually. "But no one real serious. I've told you that."

The door at the end of the corridor was open and Brett placed his arm around Kim's waist as they walked through. Kim was surprised to see such a beautiful room. The carpet was pale blue and all the furniture was a darker blue. Tables were set up at one end, containing the gifts and a selection of food and drinks.

Josie, dressed in black satin pants and a vest, came over to greet them. "Pleased you guys got here. Come and see the place, Kimmy." She grabbed her sister's hand.

Kim was dragged on a tour with her sister. Besides the large reception sitting room, there were two big bedrooms, one bathroom with a shower and basin and another with a whirlpool tub, a full-size dining room and a huge kitchen from which there was an exit to the outdoor swimming pool.

Kim touched one of the gleaming copper pots on a shelf. "Are these a wedding present?"

"No." Josie came closer. "They belong to Brett."

"He cooks?"

"Apparently." Josie ran her fingers over the surface of one of the pots. "They're almost the color of your hair, aren't they? But then Brett seems partial to copper."

Kim glanced at her sister. "What are you insinuating?"

"Brand told me that Brett has had a crush on you for years."

Kim shook her head. "No way." Yet she recalled the way he had pinpointed her sixteen-year-old self in the photograph at home. The way he had mentioned her hair color at the airport. Lots of little innuendos. But surely that was only because it was related to the last time they saw one another. She mustn't forget the disdain she had seen on his face that evening. She mustn't.

"It could be possible," Josie said.

"Even if it were, Josie, I've got . . ."

"Blah, blah, blah. I know what you've got, Kim. Can't you just see beyond that job for once?"

Kim saw tears in her sister's eyes. "I'm sorry, Josie." Kim hugged her sister. "I don't mean to be this way. But I hated Valleyview at one time and I just wanted to get away."

Josie pulled away. "I don't think you do hate it, Kim. I think that's your problem. I think you really like it and you have to pretend you don't."

Kim ran her hand over her hair. "You're probably right. I have this pull to be here, yet I don't want to be here, because I know how I feel when I am here."

"Which makes perfect sense, Kim."

Kim smiled. "Doesn't it?"

"Go look at the gifts," Josie told her. "We've got some super stuff."

Kim returned to the other room. Brett brought Liz and Frank over.

"Pleased you could make it, Kim," Frank said graciously.

Liz smiled at her. "It's nice to have you home."

"Thank you," Kim said, with a surreptitious glance at Frank. It was the first time she had seen him since her mother's admission. She could understand why her mother might fall for the man. He was handsome. Brett was very much like him.

When Kim had finished viewing the gifts, she discovered that Brett wasn't around. As everyone was still in a party mode, she left the suite and walked into the rest of the house. Kim thought Brett might be in the sitting room, but he wasn't. The glasses they had used earlier were still on the silver tray. She looked out through the windows, but the gardens were dark. Lights, beyond the row of hedges, were from the barns.

Despite what she told Brett, she felt she could easily work here. But where would she live? She didn't want to live at home with her parents. She felt they deserved to be on their own at their time of life. However, there weren't many rental places in Valleyview, although there were a few apartments above stores. She would have to live alone, but that was okay. Each day she would come to the farm and work in the office. She would be close to the horses. She was pretty sure Brett would let her ride. She bunched her fists against the glass. What was she thinking of? She had the promotion to accept.

Which she didn't want to accept. That was the trouble. She didn't want to share the position with someone else. She wanted it all. The proposed promotion had been such a bust that it was making her consider Brett's offer to come home. And if she came home, wouldn't she be giving in and admitting that she had failed in Chicago?

Could she do that? Or did she have too much pride to appear to have given in. Better to go on and do what she was doing. Maybe she would accept the promotion and look around for another position in the city. That's what she would do. That way she would still have all her pride intact. And she wouldn't have any major decisions to make. She could continue living with Hilary in her apartment. Other than her job location, nothing would change. To return to Valleyview meant too much emotional turmoil.

With that decision made, Kim returned to the apartment to find Brett still wasn't around, so she rode home with her parents, trying not to feel disappointed.

On Friday Kim got up early to help her mother with the breakfast. As not one member of the family was working today, Moira thought they should have a family sit-down meal. But Josie wasn't up to sitting down for long. Kim could see her sister was fraught with nerves. Kim decided to take charge. She dealt with an emergency over the flowers and took Josie's car to pick up their dresses from Isobel. Then when she returned, she helped Josie pack for her honeymoon.

They went as a family in Allan's car to the rehearsal in the small whitewashed church. Kim didn't know the minister. He was new in town and met them in the church, and about ten minutes later the Stanton family arrived. Kim surreptitiously looked at Brett. She couldn't help it. His good looks took her breath away. It seemed he could wear a plain gray suit in a different way than most men. Even the white shirt and striped tie appeared different on him. His hair was thick and shiny, brushing his collar. While his features were smooth and he looked clean-shaven and fresh, she thought his eyes seemed a little dark, as if he hadn't been sleeping too well.

When he found her watching him, he met her

glance and pursed his lips rather cynically; it made her remember his kiss last night by the stairs. He seemed to make the decision to come over to join her. "I see you are as uptight as ever," he said softly.

She met his green gaze. "What do you mean by that?"

"Well, last night you let loose in orange. Now you're back in your basic black business suit with your hair in a bun. At Deanna's I thought for sure, if the group became silent, I would hear your nerves screech like a set of car tires cornering too fast."

"I wore it loose last night, but you lost interest in me partway through the evening." She really hadn't meant to say that but it had seemed that way.

"I went to have a look at an ailing horse."

"Oh." She felt bad because she had thought she was the excuse for his leaving. "I'm sorry. Is it okay?"

"Yes. It'll be okay. But we had a couple of worrying moments."

"One of the important horses?"

"They're all important to me, Kim. No, it was one of the riding horses. But he'll be fine. Thanks for being concerned." Brett smiled, his teeth white and dazzling.

Kim couldn't tear her gaze away from him. They stared at one another and she felt the beat of their attraction mounting. Josie was right. There was something. But of course, she knew it. She had known it from the moment she had stared across the airport and seen him, known it the moment he strode toward her and clasped her hand firmly in his.

"Next time," she said. "Tell me."

He lowered his head slightly as he often did, and it appeared so intimate to her. "Tell you what?"

"Tell me if you're leaving. I could have helped with the horse." Or helped you cope, she thought. Oh, what was she thinking? She didn't want to be involved with him. But she was involved with him.

"Hoping there aren't many next times, but knowing there probably will be, I'll let you know. However, does that offer mean you're considering staying?"

He didn't miss opportunities. Kim shook her head. "Oh, I didn't really mean it that way. I have to go back to Chicago, obviously."

"But you are weighing the pros and cons?"

"Naturally, I would. If it would further my career, then it would be a benefit to me."

"Well, I suppose I can't ask for more than

that." He glanced around, then took hold of her elbow. "Come on. Wedding rehearsal time."

Kim felt nervous about walking down the aisle to where Brand and Brett stood. But after they went through the motions twice, and she got used to accepting Josie's imaginary bouquet and holding onto Brett's arm as they returned down the aisle, she was feeling more confident about the real thing tomorrow. Even if Brett did tuck her hand more firmly down beside his arm until she felt warm and wanted. Even if his smile seemed to light something up inside her and make her warm all through.

Frank Stanton was hosting a dinner at a restaurant just outside town for the remainder of the evening. It was an expensive, exclusive place Kim had never been to before. But she didn't show that she was impressed. She kept her head held high and acted as if restaurants with waiters dancing to serve her every whim were a normal everyday occurrence for her.

Brett sat down beside her, and that made sense really, she decided, arranging the linen napkin on her lap that had been lavishly placed there by one waiter. After all, everyone else was a couple. Brett and Kim were the odd ones out, paired together for the wedding.

"Nice place?" Brett said, looking around.

"Usual fare for you, I should imagine," she quipped.

"Cut it out," he said between his teeth. "I'm sure you've been to a few places like this in Chicago."

"Occasionally. Yes."

"Business?"

"Mostly."

His shoulder touched hers. "She won't admit to letting loose and having fun, will she?"

"There hasn't been much time, Brett."

"Well, there is time now. An entire weekend of time. So be good, Kim. For Josie's sake. I like your sister. I find her extremely beautiful and vulnerable. I hope my brother is good to her. No, more than good. I hope he cherishes her."

She met his glittery gaze. "Is that how you would treat your wife? I mean, when you find that special someone."

"Definitely."

The attraction pulsed between them once more. Kim dragged her eyes away from him and picked up the menu that had been placed before her. She buried her face in it, all the print blurring before her eyes.

"What are you going to have?"

"I don't know yet."

He shoved his knee hard against hers. "Kim."

Kim felt very weak from the pressure of his warm vital leg pushed against hers. "What are you doing?"

He turned to her and reached out. Carefully he tugged a few hairs from above her ears and drew the curls down the side of her face, just the way Josie had done the other day, except Kim's heart was pounding so hard she could barely think. "That's better," he said. "It makes you look softer."

His touch made her tremble. His heady gaze made her breathless. She quickly chose chicken and told the waiter when he came to ask, pleased for a moment to turn her attention away from Brett.

After that the meal seemed to go smoothly. They didn't hang around too long, since everyone needed their beauty sleep. Outside the restaurant, Brett tugged Brand away from Josie.

"Cool it, you two, you're not supposed to see one another on your wedding day and if we stay out any longer, it will be *the* day."

Brett trundled Brand off, and Josie and Kim climbed into their dad's car, both laughing. When they got home, Kim went up to bed, while Josie stayed up to check the weather forecast for Sat-

urday. Promised, she heard Josie call out exuber-
antly, was a sunny summery day. Kim smiled. It
would be fine. She would do everything she could
to help make it fine.

Chapter Seven

Kim peered around the door into the church. It was decorated in wedding style with white bows and ribbons and masses of flowers. She couldn't believe so many people sat on Josie's side of the church. But why couldn't she believe it? Did she really think her family was so down the class scale that they had no friends in Valleyview? Swallowing hard, Kim glanced at her fragrant bouquet of roses. She realized now, and was becoming to realize it more and more, that she had always equated her family with the Stanton family, when in fact there were many families in Valleyview, most of them on the same economic level as her own, that they should be equated with. Some were even above their economic level. Tyler Matheson, Josie's employer, and his wife, Dahlia, kept glancing back expectantly to see Josie.

And then there were relatives. They didn't have a huge family, but her mother's sister, Charlene, was here with her husband, plus two female cousins from Florida, who had been the children of the uncle with the riding school. They were older than Kim, both in their thirties and unmarried career women, whom she quite admired. Grandma Mason, her mother's mother, had also been brought in from a Louisville retirement home to see her granddaughter married.

One of the ushers, a handsome college friend of Brand's, touched Kim's arm.

"Kim. You're on after Stephanie."

"Thanks."

It was Stephanie, acting as flower girl, who broke the ice. The entire church burst into chatter, flashing camera bulbs, and smiles as they glimpsed the little girl in a dress of lemon-mist chiffon, with flowers and ribbons in her long black hair.

Kim glanced back at Josie and her father before she took her walk. "Good luck, you guys."

Josie let out a shaky breath. "Don't trip."

"You neither. See you down there." Kim smiled. Josie looked like an angel with her blond hair upswept and lots of ringlets cascading down her cheeks.

Kim began to pace her walk down the aisle. Faces turned in her direction, but she was really only aware of the two men waiting for her to arrive at her destination.

She realized afterward, she didn't recall the actual ceremony, but she knew it went well. She did remember signing the wedding certificate in the back room. She also recalled Brett's firm arm moving her to the door to make the trip back up the aisle. And she definitely recalled her fingers clutching the smooth material of his black tuxedo and sensing the strength of his muscles beneath. She had never thought she needed the support of a man before, but in those few moments she needed Brett's.

In the sparkling sunshine photographs were taken by the professional hired photographer and the amateurs. The bride and groom were so happy and in love that everyone bathed in their joy. Family secrets were forgotten today.

"Stick with me," Brett said, still holding her hand on his arm, rubbing her fingers occasionally as if he felt she needed to be brought to life.

"Where else would I go?" she asked, rolling her eyes. "We have more official photographs in the gardens, don't we?"

"Yes. Then the reception, which will be quite a party. Some of Brand's friends can get rowdy."

Kim glanced at the group of young men, some with pretty young women who were wives and girlfriends, all handsome, well-groomed, and already having a great time. "I can see they might."

"Too close to college age," Brett remarked.

"And you're not, of course?"

He made a face. "Like you, it was a while back."

"Are you saying I'm on the maturing side of twenty-five?"

"Well, aren't you?" He grinned.

"Yes," she admitted, returning his smile. "But I'm not old."

"I never said you were. I'm older than you."

"Not much."

"No. Although it seemed older when I was eighteen and you were sixteen, but now it seems perfectly respectable that we should be together."

Kim didn't have time to dwell on his comment because Aunt Charlene and Uncle Roy and her cousins came over to see her. She introduced Julianne and Patricia and her aunt and uncle to Brett, and she could see they were all very impressed with him.

"Are you the next bride?" Aunt Charlene asked in an aside to Kim.

"Oh, I don't think so. He's just acting as my escort."

"I'd snap him up," Charlene told her. "Wow."

Kim laughed. Charlene looked like her mother, but she was much less uptight than Moira.

Finally Kim and Brett were alone again.

"Let's go," Brett said. "I'm getting thirsty, and it looks as if there is another wedding due."

He led her to his Mercedes and made sure she was neatly tucked into the front seat. Kim didn't usually like men fussing around her, but she quite liked Brett doing this for her today. It was a little old-fashioned chivalry that a lot of men she knew didn't bother with anymore. Besides, in her long pretty dress, she felt old-fashioned.

She studied him as he drove. His skin was smoothly shaven and his hair touched the crisp white collar of his shirt.

He glanced at her. "Do I pass?"

"Yes." She felt like touching him, so she kept her fingers firmly around her bouquet. He had worked enough magic on her that this day was going to be a special memory for her. She only hoped she could keep the magic confined to this one day, to enable her to return to Chicago intact.

"You pass as well. You look beautiful."

She touched her hair, professionally styled this morning by Josie's stylist. A coronet of roses had been placed upon the hairdo. "Thank you." It was all she could say.

His fingers gripped the steering wheel. "Save me a slow dance?"

"Of course. You've been a great help to me today. You kept me upright when I would have stumbled."

"I wasn't that steady myself." He shifted in his seat. "You think it's not going to bother you, a wedding, especially your brother's, but it does. It's quite emotional."

"It is," Kim agreed, quite surprised to find Brett admitting to emotional frailty. It made him human, a real person, not just a mythical Stanton man. "They are a lovely couple though."

"I think they'll make it," he said.

Kim crossed her fingers. She had one or two school friends who hadn't made it much past the wedding day. Josie was too full of hope to have her dreams dashed.

Brett drove through the gates of Stanton Farm, where already some limousines were parked and guest cars lined up. He continued along the road that went to the stables. A row of garages belonging to the house stood in a line. He opened one with an automatic opener and they drove inside.

"Save some of the parking space," he said, stopping the car and turning off the engine.

The door slid down behind them making the area dark. Kim gathered her little silver purse and her flowers together. Brett stopped her from leaving the car by placing his arm around her shoulders.

"One thing," he said softly.

Kim met his eyes that were dark in the dim light, and he slanted his mouth over hers and gave her a brief but tantalizing kiss. "For a beautiful bridesmaid. Catch the bouquet—you might be the next bride."

"No way," she said. "I like being a career woman." But the words weren't sounding quite as positive as they used to. Maybe because she used to mean them. Now she wasn't so sure.

Brett got out of the car and came around to help Kim again. They walked through a door into a spacious mud room. Coats hung from hooks, and a row of boots stood on the floor beneath a bench. It was also an entrance to the house from the stables. They had come through here the morning they had gone horseback riding together. Kim thought that morning seemed a long time ago now, yet it was only a handful of days.

"Do you want to freshen up?" Brett asked, indicating a powder room off the mud room.

"I think I might," Kim told him. "I'll meet you outside."

"Okay. I'll be there in a while."

Kim shut the powder room door behind her and let out a long breath. Brett's kisses were beginning to work a spell on her. She was almost in love with him. Or was she already in love with him? She didn't want to answer that question today. She felt she should merely have a good time and worry about answers tomorrow.

Straightening her shoulders, Kim walked to the mirror. She put on some coral lipstick and a little eye shadow for the photographs. Then she made her way through the house and out the glass door of the sitting room into the gardens.

Two white marquees had been erected. Inside they were set up with a bar and tables for the meal. A crowd was already gathering on the lawn. A high-end crowd, Kim noted by the styles of pastel clothes and big hats on the women and expensive suits on the men. They all looked as if they were spending a day at the races. Josie came over to grab Kim for the photographs, which were to be taken in the spring garden. Brett was already there organizing the photographer.

After the photographs, Kim lost track of Brett. She chatted with her mother and father and Charlene and Roy for a while, and then sat with her

Gran. Gran tended to ramble on a bit, and she was never quite sure which of the girls was Kim or Josie.

"You are a lovely bride," Gran said, patting Kim's hand with her thin fingers.

"Josie is the bride, Gran," she said. "I still live in Chicago."

"You're not marrying the brother?"

"No. No. We're just together because of the wedding."

"Handsome boys." Gran leaned forward. "Always were handsome, the Stanton boys. I knew Frank's father, you know."

Kim wasn't surprised. Everyone in Valleyview knew the Stantons. "Did you know him well?"

Gran's eyes twinkled. "Very well. But I met your grandfather and married him instead."

"You mean, you had a chance to marry a Stanton?"

"I could have married one," Gran said, patting her coiffured silver hair. "I got your mother the job here with Frank. But she didn't seem to like it much. She didn't stay very longs."

"No. Well, it was a lot of work looking after this big house."

"Yes, I suppose." Gran faded off.

"Do you want me to get you a cup of tea, Gran?"

"No." She pulled Kim's arm forward. "I'd like a beer."

"Gran?"

"Get me one, Kim. This is a wedding."

"All right I'll get you one."

Kim met Brett by the bar.

"Ready to drink the night away?" he asked.

"No. My Gran wants a beer."

He laughed. "Really? The little white-haired lady with the cane?"

"Yes."

"I'll get her one. What do you want?"

"A glass of white wine would be nice, Brett."

It didn't take him long to get their drinks. He carried them on a tray over to her Gran.

"Oh, thank you, son," Gran said, taking the beer. "Now you two come and sit down and tell me all about your plans for your honeymoon."

Brett glanced at Kim. Kim mouthed, "She gets me mixed up with Josie."

He nodded and sat down with Gran. Kim sat on the other side, holding her glass.

He clicked his beer glass against her grandmother's. "To your good health," he said and Kim saw him smile as Gran put away half her glass of beer in one gulp.

"Now you tell me about your honeymoon and where you are going to live when you get back."

"We're not getting married, Gran. It's Josie and Brett's brother, Brand, who are married."

Gran looked at Brett. "And you're not?"

"Not yet," Brett said, glancing at Kim with a mischievous glint in his eye. "But just wait."

"Well, I hope you do get married. I love weddings." Gran finished her beer. "That was good." She handed her glass to Brett. "Can I have another?"

Brett got another glass but Kim noticed there was less beer in it than the previous one. She gave him a grateful look. Then, leaving Gran contented, Brett escorted Kim around to introduce her to the Stanton friends, who were mostly wealthy horse people from Canada, New York, California, and Florida—even two couples from England. There were also Stanton relatives from different parts of the country, and Brand's own acquaintances. Kim also got stopped by one or two old friends of her parents.

"It seems like a lot of people are going to stay on for the Derby," she said to Brett.

"Yes, I know. Can you come home for that?"

"No way. I've used up all my vacation for a while."

"How about the Breeders Cup in the autumn?"

"I don't know. I have the new job."

He shoved his hands into his pockets. "My job

would be different. I would let you off for Derby Day and the Breeders. You could even come with me to other races. Belmont, Saratoga. It would be fun."

Kim raised an eyebrow. "You mean, if I worked for you?"

"Yes. That's what I'm saying." He shrugged and smiled. "I'm just trying to put some icing on the cake. That's all."

"I have to admit it's tasty," she told him. "But I really should stay where I am."

Kim didn't think he was too pleased with that answer and after a while they drifted apart again. Kim made a friend of the blond-haired handsome usher. His name was Greg Morehead. By the time dinner was announced, Greg was ready to make her his partner for the evening. She saw Brett watch Greg pull out her chair for her at the table. He was sitting the other side of Brand. She was sitting beside Josie.

Josie leaned over. "Seems like Greg has a soft spot for you. Brett might get jealous."

"There's nothing to be jealous about."

"I'm not so sure. He looks as if he swallowed a black cloud."

Kim surreptitiously glanced at Brett. He did look rather grumpy. She shrugged her shoulders.

"I don't know why. We've been together quite a bit."

After dinner the speeches began, and Brett's story about his brother was both poignant and funny. When Brand had been quite small he used to chase horse's tails. Brett had always found this dangerous and watched in case his little brother ever got kicked, which he miraculously didn't. It was Brett who had almost been trampled by a rearing horse. Brand had put himself in danger to save Brett from being trampled. Kim was taken from laughter to tears all in a matter of minutes. What if Brand hadn't saved Brett's life? She didn't even want to think about that scenario. She could see Liz felt the same way as she glanced at her elder son, and Kim felt a wrench to her heart.

As soon as the meal was over, a band set up and dancing began. After the bride and groom had danced the initial waltz, Greg was ready to make Kim his partner.

"Are you with Brett?" Greg asked as they waltzed around the patio.

"Oh, not really," she told him. "We were just together because of the wedding. It's all over now."

"Great. Do you live around here?"

"No. I live in Chicago."

"Hey, so do I. I work downtown. Do you work downtown?"

"Yes. I do."

"We'll do lunch then, Kim."

Greg was maybe a year younger than her, but what did it matter. Why not do lunch with him one day? She had promised herself she would now eat lunch.

"I work in advertising," she told him. "What about you?"

"Money," he said with a rise of one eyebrow. "What else is there today?"

"Horses."

"That's Brand's specialty. I met him in college and that's how I got to know him. I don't know anything about horses. While the breeding side seems more profitable than the racing, too many ifs with animals involved for my liking."

"Then you don't ride or anything?"

His expression was comical. "Think you could get me on top of a horse? No way."

Maybe she wouldn't do lunch with him, Kim thought when she made an excuse to use the powder room. They would be completely incompatible. She went into the house and through to the sitting room, where she sat down in one of the wing armchairs. She really did like men of the land, she thought. She really did.

"Are you sleeping?"

She looked up to see Brett hunkering down, holding on to the arms of the chair. His hair was a little less sleek now from the rigors of the day, and his tie was loosened and awry.

"No. I'm not sleeping."

"But you needed a rest from all the excitement, I bet. I thought you'd disappeared with Morehead?"

"No. We only danced."

"Is he your type?"

She had to be honest. She shook her head. "No."

Brett nodded. "That's not what I would have thought."

She met his gaze. "Because you don't know me, even if you think you do."

He shook his head. "You promised me a slow dance."

"You've got a one-track mind."

"I know. For the past week it's been on you."

"Only because you've been forced into my company."

"You think that's the reason?"

"Yes. I do."

"Then you don't know me, either. Come on." He took hold of her hands and lifted her to her feet.

They walked to the patio and Brett closed his arms around her, the way he had in the blues club the other evening. His steady heartbeat pounded beneath her palm.

"Gran's watching you," he said softly. "She thinks we make a good couple."

Why was he doing this? Was he swept away in the emotion of the day? She had to go away on Tuesday morning. Really, there was no point in letting go with Brett.

They danced four slow dances, then moved into fast dances. All Brand's friends were on the dance floor with them. The bride had removed her shoes and her veil was flying as she twisted and turned. Brand's white shirtsleeves were rolled up. His hair lay plastered to his head with sweat.

Brett danced Kim close to the newly married couple. "You'll wear yourself out for your wedding night," Brett said.

Josie grinned. "We'll be on the plane tonight."

"I envy you going to Barbados. I loved it there," Kim told her.

"I'm intending to love it as well," Josie said.

"We'll have a great time," Brand said. "I haven't been there either, so we can discover it together."

"Sweet young love," Brett purred with a smile.

"It is," Josie said, giving her new husband a hug.

Her sister's rings glittered, and Kim buried her gaze against Brett's shoulder. For a second, she actually felt jealous of Josie's love.

When the dancing was over, Kim went to the guest apartment with her mother to help Josie prepare to leave. Josie put on a pair of ivory silk slacks and a jacket.

"You didn't catch my bouquet, Kimmy."

"No. One of your friend's girlfriends did."

Josie rolled her eyes. "Sounds like another wedding then. Did you have fun?"

"Great fun," Kim said.

"Mom?" Josie asked.

Moira sniffed and Kim saw her mother was crying.

"It was fantastic, Josie. Now you have fun on your vacation, won't you?"

"Of course I will, Mom."

They both clutched each other, crying, and Kim knew they were closer because Josie had never left home. Kim had become the strong one; Josie was the little one still.

Josie turned to Kim for a hug. When they pulled apart, Josie said, "My car keys are on the hook in the kitchen. You can use my car until you leave."

"Thank you," Kim said. Having wheels would enable her to get around. She wouldn't have to rely on the Stantons.

The newlyweds left in a stretch white limousine with everyone waving and taking photographs. Afterward the guests continued to enjoy themselves. Children were still dancing, including a lot of young adults. Her father took Gran home to their house to stay the night. Charlene and Roy were in a motel, but Patricia and Julianne had decided they would stay as well to look after Gran, so Allan took them home too. However, her mother stayed on and Kim couldn't believe her eyes when she saw Moira dancing with Frank.

She turned away and bumped into Greg. He grasped her waist. "Hey, I've been looking for you to dance again."

Kim let herself be taken on to the dance floor again. Everyone was quite wild this late at night, letting down their hair in every respect. Even after ten minutes with Greg on the dance floor, Frank and Moira were still there. Her father hadn't returned. Brett was missing. Deanna was sipping a soda while watching the dancing, and Kim wasn't sure if she was watching her father, or her daughter dancing with a bunch of other kids.

She wondered why they had to dance together? Had they talked about the past at all? Was Frank still in love with Moira? If so, would that cause even more problems?

Greg grasped her hand. "Kim you keep wandering away from me."

"I don't feel too good," she half-fibbed. "I think I need a rest."

He wasn't happy to let her go, but five minutes later she saw him with another woman. She still couldn't see Brett anywhere, and she wished she could, because she wanted to go home.

But she couldn't go home. She didn't have any transportation and it was too far to walk in high heels at this time of night. She saw Deanna coming over to her.

"Hi, Kim, I've hardly seen you today. What did you think of the wedding?"

"Wonderful," Kim said. "They seem really happy."

"Yes, they do. I think my brother will make a good husband." Deanna's gaze went to the dance floor. "Our families seem to be getting along."

Kim followed her glance to Moira and Frank. Her throat choked. "Yes, they do," she said huskily.

"That's good. We wouldn't want tension, would we? How's it going with Brett?"

"Fine. He's gone now. I mean, the wedding's over. His duties are finished."

"How are you getting home then?"

"Probably with my dad. He'll be back. He took Gran and some cousins home."

"Okay." Deanna smiled. "Stephie's really looking forward to your ride tomorrow."

"Great." Kim forced a bright smile. "That's wonderful."

Deanna wandered away and Kim turned around to see her father walk back on to the lawn. She also noticed that her mother had left Frank. Frank was now with Liz. Moira came over to Kim and Allan.

"I think I would like to call it a night," Moira said. "It's been an emotional day."

"I'll take you home," Allan said. "Gran's in Josie's room. Julie and Pat are in the living room on the sofa bed, so we're a full house. Are you coming with us, Kim?"

"Yes, I will. I'll just say goodnight to Brett if I can find him."

She found him in the sitting room in the same wing chair she had been sitting in earlier. He had a seltzer on the table beside him.

"Fed up with socializing?" she asked.

"Yeah. How about you?"

"I'm going home. Dad came back."

"Okay I'll see you tomorrow then. We probably won't ride until afternoon. Say two at the stables?"

"Yes. I'll be there." She couldn't get out of it. She couldn't disappoint Stephanie. But that wasn't all. She couldn't disappoint herself.

All the way home in the car, she realized now what had happened. She had fallen in love with Brett and he had turned cool to her now that his wedding duties were over. She had been a first-class fool.

Chapter Eight

"I thought it was a success," Allan said as the family car swished smoothly through town.

"Oh, definitely," Moira told him and looked at Kim. "Don't you think so?"

"It was great," Kim said, even though she thought her mother might have exacerbated her problems by dancing with Frank and letting everyone see them together. Or maybe that was their way of saying that nothing was going on anymore, that it was all over, and that they were friends? She hoped it was the latter and everything was cool between the families now.

Sunday morning dawned a little dull and rainy. The house seemed packed with her cousins and Gran, who needed quite a bit of attention, but she also seemed to be enjoying herself.

"I thought you got married yesterday?" she asked Kim, when Kim poured herself a cup of coffee.

"No. That was Josie, Gran."

"But weren't you with a handsome Stanton man?"

"She sure was," Patricia piped up. "Brett Stanton. Gorgeous, gorgeous, gorgeous."

Julianne glanced at Kim. "Are you going out with him?"

"No. I live in Chicago. I don't live here."

"But we would like her back," Moira inserted. "Wouldn't we, Dad?"

Allan shook his head. "Only if she wants to come. She's grown up now, Mom."

"Yes, I'm grown up." She smiled rather mischievously at her family. "But I'm still going riding with Brett this afternoon."

Patricia pretended to swoon.

"And his ten-year-old niece."

"That's okay, Kim," Julianne said. "I would use any excuse to get close to that man."

Brett phoned her about noon inquiring about her transportation to the farm. She told she had Josie's car at her disposal so she could be there and he didn't have to bother fetching her.

"Sure?"

"I'm sure. You have to pick up Stephie, don't you?"

"No. She stayed the night here. It gives Deanna and Gordon some time alone."

"They're getting along fine now, though?"

"Who told you there were problems? Probably, Josie. Yep. Things seem to be improving. And, by the way, I talked to Dad."

Kim's throat suddenly closed up. "Yes."

"Everything's fine. They had a talk and that's it. It's all forgiven and forgotten. So now *you* can forget it."

"All right. Great. That's good." Kim saw her mother in the doorway. "Anyway, I'll see you at the stables, Brett." As Kim hung up the phone, she couldn't help but say softly, "Brett said you've made peace."

Moira nodded. "Yes, we did. Don't worry anymore. It's past, it's over. Really over."

"I'm pleased, Mom."

"So am I," Moira said. "In fact, I think Josie did me a favor. Now go and enjoy your ride with Brett."

"You didn't want me to get involved with him."

Moira shook her head. "It doesn't matter what you do, honey. Just have some fun."

Kim tugged a denim jacket over a T-shirt and

jeans. She drew her hair back from her face, then stopped herself. Instead, she tucked on a wide-brimmed white riding hat she had at the top of her closet. It suited her and it would keep off the persistent drizzle.

As she passed the house and went to the barn, Kim realized she had never actually physically driven in through the gates of Stanton Farm by herself before. She parked the car in front of the paddock and pocketed the keys as she got out. Stephanie, in boots, jeans, a windbreaker jacket, and a hat similar to Kim's, ran over to her.

"Hey, Kim. Uncle Brett will be here in a moment. He told me to tell you. The horses are ready." Stephie grabbed hold of Kim's hand. "Come on."

Brett showed up a few moments later in his jeans, gray hooded sweatshirt, and denim jacket.

"Not hung over?" he asked Kim.

She smiled. "No. I barely drink. What about you?"

"Me also," he said.

Stephie pulled his arm. "Uncle Brett, let's get going."

"All right, sweetie." He gave his niece a hug and swung her around a bit. She screamed with laughter.

Kim found it wasn't the same type of ride

she'd had with Brett the first time. Stephanie kept everything on a level, and they all ended up joining into her conversation about frogs, trees, horses, kids at school, anything that popped into her head. She saw everything with new eyes, and Kim began to enjoy her company. She glanced over at Brett and wondered what it would be like to be married to him and have a little girl like Stephanie between them.

Come on, Kim, you'll never be the woman for him. What are you thinking about? Just because he showed courtesy during the wedding doesn't mean to say he could love you. Whatever Josie thinks.

When the ride was over they played with some newborn kittens, then they ate a casual early dinner in the Stanton kitchen. Kim could tell Stephanie was used to this treatment. Uncle Brett was her idol. As Kim had Josie's car, there was no ride home with Brett. She went home alone to find her mother and father getting ready to take Gran back. Julianne and Patricia would fly out tomorrow morning. As Kim spent the rest of the day with her cousins, it seemed like time had flown by. One more day and she returned to her job, her new job.

After her cousins had left on Monday, Kim packed her own suitcase. She had to get her mind

ready to go back to Chicago. She also had to tell
John her decision. She paced for a long time.
Should she? Shouldn't she? Then she decided she
should. Just because she had been home for a
week, didn't mean to say she should be swayed
to stay here. Especially by a Stanton, although,
she had to admit she didn't feel quite so down
on the family anymore. They had been generous
to her family for the wedding. Everyone had done
their best to make Josie and Brand happy.

Mid-morning she picked up the phone in the
dining room and called John. She told him that
she would accept the position, even if she was
disappointed about the share situation.

"We did that because Rosemary has found the
position has become larger over the years. Lorne
is on the same level as you and ready for a promotion, so we thought, why not, for a while, see
how a shared managerial position would work.
It's to alleviate stress, Kim."

"I understand." *But I wanted more,* she
thought. *I wanted it all.*

"But we'll definitely review the position in six
months, Kim."

Her next phone call came from Brett. He
wanted to take her for dinner at the B&B as he
had promised.

"I have a date with Brett," she told her mother, when Moira inquired about the evening meal.

"A date?" Moira asked.

Kim nodded. "He wants to fatten me up so he's taking me out to dinner."

Moira smiled. "Well, I suppose that is a good excuse."

"What do you mean by that?"

"I think he likes you. Josie thought he did."

Kim shook her head. "No. I think he just felt responsible for me because of the wedding. This will be goodbye tonight."

"Not goodbye forever, I hope. Now things are better for us, you will come home more often."

"That wasn't the reason I stayed away, Mom."

Moira raised both eyebrows. "Tell me another one."

"Okay. Partly, I suppose. Yes. I'll come home more often."

"Good. Now, let us take you to the airport to-morrow morning, won't you?"

"Of course, Mom."

For her evening out with Brett Kim decided to wear the orange outfit again. She left her hair loose and put on a pair of silver earrings. She heard Brett arrive, heard him go to the kitchen, and knew he would sit down and talk to her parents. Was she getting used to him coming here now? She must be. She didn't seem to mind that he was here. She didn't feel that inferior feeling anymore. Maybe because she knew him better. Josie had done her a favor as well.

When she went down to the kitchen he was seated at the table, dressed quite casually in a sports jacket over slacks, shirt and tie. But whatever he wore, his appearance took her breath away.

Covering her breathlessness with a smile, she said, "I'm ready."

He looked at her long and hard before he rose from the chair. "I like you in orange."

"It should clash with her hair," Allan said. "But it doesn't, does it?"

Brett glanced at her father. "Who had hair that color in your family?"

"My mother," Allan said. "She died a few years ago. She was very silver by then."

Kim rolled her eyes. "Which means I'll turn silver."

"Not for a long time," her mother said. "Have a good time you two."

They walked to the restaurant. Kim thought Brett seemed a bit withdrawn as soon as they were alone together. She had to admit she felt a bit withdrawn herself. Tomorrow she would leave Valleyview, and although it wasn't that far from,

Chicago in miles, it was still a distance. It was so different in the city.

"Did you make a decision as to your job?" he asked.

"Yes. I accepted."

"That's good then. So if you hear of a really good graphic artist who wants my job offer, then you can pass them on."

"I will." But she didn't like the vision of another woman working with Brett. Although, one day she would probably have to get used to him with a woman, when he got married. She might even have to attend his wedding.

They sat by a window overlooking the gardens again. This time they had a roast beef dinner, which was the specialty on Monday evenings.

"Promise me you'll eat lunches from now on," Brett said as they ate.

Kim sipped her water. "I've promised myself I will. I agree with you, I was beginning to stress out."

"I guess that's what it was. It's all that climbing and clawing."

She smiled. "Did I really tell you that?"

"Yes. You did. You had a real heavy burden on your shoulders when you first arrived."

"I've changed my mind a little," she admitted.

"How come?"

"Oh, just seeing that you work hard and that you haven't been spoon-fed everything helped."

"You really saw our families as them and us, didn't you?"

"Probably because mother worked for your father."

"Even if he did fall in love with her?"

"It was probably just infatuation."

"Do you know the difference between real love and infatuation?"

"Do you?"

"You always turn questions around to suit yourself? I want to know what you think about love."

"It's not for me, I don't think. I don't like hurting."

"So you'll never get married?"

"I can't say never, but not in the immediate future."

"Me neither, probably." Brett picked up his water glass. "Anyway, let me propose a toast to Kim and her new promotion and hope that everything goes well for you, honey."

Tears welled in Kim's eyes. This was it. She wouldn't see Brett again for a while. Maybe next time she came to Valleyview, she would go to Stanton Farm to visit Josie and he might be there. What if he found the woman to light his fire in the meantime? Was she stupid not to take the job he offered so she could stay closer to him?

"Thank you, Brett," she said huskily. "I hope everything goes well for you as well. Your parents will be gone soon and you'll be in charge."

"I know. It's daunting, isn't it?"

"It's certainly a challenge. But you'll be with the horses . . ." She bit into her lip. She didn't like emotional moments.

"When you come home," he said. "You can ride any time you want."

"Thank you." She didn't add, *I will*. She wasn't sure if she would be able to be near him in the future. She had stood on the edge of that canyon at the beginning of last week and now she had plummeted to the bottom. She needed to leave Valleyview fast.

They walked back home in the dark. Next weekend was the Derby. Lots going on. Valleyview would probably be buzzing with a few tourists. But she mustn't think of that. She had a job requiring a great deal of concentration.

When they reached her porch, she turned to Brett and went to shake his hand. "Thank you for all your help during the wedding."

He didn't let her shake his hand. "Put your arms around my neck and kiss me like you mean it."

"Oh no, Brett. I don't want to start anything I can't finish."

"What do you mean by that?"

"I'm leaving in the morning. Please, let me be."

He drew in a breath. "Who's taking you to the airport?"

"My mom and dad."

"Okay." He plunged his hands into his pockets. "Great. I'll see you next time you come home."

"Thank you for dinner."

"We'll do it next time." Then he turned and ran down the porch steps. His black Mercedes was parked in the parking area. He got inside, closed the door and started the engine. Kim watched the lights disappear down the road and then went into the house. She was pleased her parents weren't still up because all she wanted to do was go up to her room and cry.

"What's the matter?" Hilary asked as they rushed around their small kitchen putting dinner into the microwave. It was leftover chicken and lasagna from the night before.

Kim made a face as she chopped up a quick salad. "Oh, this promotion isn't working out. Lorne acts like the boss and bosses me around. And I'm supposed to be his equal."

Hilary tossed back her mane of dark hair. "Then you'll have to talk to him about it, won't you?"

"Or quit."

Hilary put two bowls out for the salad. "You'd quit C&C after you've worked this hard to get where you are?"

"Where am I, though?" Kim complained. "I'm one slot up from where I was before. I'm in a share position. The raise was minimal. I can't move from here with it. I thought . . ." She clucked her tongue. "I thought it would be better than this."

"They've messed you around, haven't they?"

"Yes. And now I'm beginning to think they did the same thing to Rosemary Tilbury. When she left she was relieved. She was going to work at home with her husband. They're starting a business. They've had enough of not seeing one another or their son. So they both quit their jobs. It's a gamble, but she says they have to be happier than they were."

"Yes. But she has the support of a man and the marriage," Hilary said. "You're single."

"I know. That's why I have to do better than I am right now."

Hilary took the bowls of salad and put them on the table. She added cutlery. The microwave pinged and Kim removed their heated food. She put the dish on the kitchen table, peeled off the plastic wrap and let the steam escape. Hilary sat down opposite her. They both began to dig in hungrily.

"If I don't want that job I have to quit, Hilary. That's the way things work there."

"I know. I'm sure you'll find another job. I hope you do because things went really well for me at home, and Paul is coming to Chicago for a while to see me."

"Oh, Hilary, that's great. When?"

"He'll be here this weekend."

"Wonderful. So it's serious?"

"It always has been for him apparently."

"And you didn't know?"

Hilary shook her head. "He never let on. He said he let me go free first otherwise I wouldn't have had a chance to pursue my broadcasting career when I had the opportunity."

"He's in TV, isn't he?"

"He's a cameraman. We're in the same line of work."

"I hope it works out for you, Hilary. You are in love with him?"

Hilary nodded. "Oh, yes. But I didn't really know it until I went back to New York."

The same way she hadn't known about love

until she went back to Valleyview, Kim thought, as she walked through the swing doors of the big office tower the next morning. She missed Brett desperately. Not that it did her any good loving Brett. He hadn't contacted her since she had left Valleyview. Her mother had told her on the phone she had talked to him once in town when she saw him at Gina's bookstore. And of course, Josie had arrived back a few days ago.

"She looks great," Moira said to Kim on the phone the other evening. "They seem so happy and suited for one another."

Kim jammed her finger on the elevator button. She had probably been in love with Brett all of her life. Or at least since she was sixteen. She just hadn't realized that love until she had been with him again. She leaned against the back of the elevator car as it traveled to the fifteenth floor. She wasn't looking forward to another day at C&C.

The company had given her a separate office from Lorne, but she still wasn't satisfied. Lorne, who was a thin man in glasses, was domineering. He made the decisions. He never asked her opinion, never wanted to know if they could compromise. He was opinionated and always right.

At lunch she was meeting a friend from another advertising agency. She would check if there were any positions. And then there is always Brett's offer, she told herself. But could she handle loving Brett and working for him at the same time? If she had really lit his fire during the week of the wedding, wouldn't he have contacted her?

Lorne was waiting in her office after lunch. He was looking through some of her work.

"Hi," he said as she walked around her desk. "Have you seen this work of Paula's? It's terrible."

"I haven't. I asked her to leave me proofs. Lorne please let me see that."

He handed her the proofs. She glanced at them. She wasn't going to make any comments. She had discovered that Lorne had been dating Paula, and Paula had turned him down a few times in the past month, so he was being overly critical.

"I'll look them over on the weekend," she said.

"Okay, whatever, but don't be easy on her."

Kim made a face at his back and slipped the proofs into her briefcase that was down beside her desk. She was collecting work for the weekend. She was taking home one of the company laptops to work on. But first she was going to hunt around for a tennis partner this evening. She needed to work off a lot of energy.

She picked up the phone and made half a

dozen calls. Each woman she called had a date that evening. *What's with this coupling?* she wondered. She put down the receiver. Well, she had plenty of work to do. She didn't have time for tennis anyway.

Her trip home was on a crushed bus. She walked the last half mile and climbed the steps to the apartment. She unlocked the door. She tossed her briefcase beside her desk, saw the answer machine flashing, but didn't bother with it then. She found a written message from Hilary to say she was out with Paul. Without removing her high heels or her suit jacket, Kim slumped on the tweed couch. She rubbed her eyes and her fingers came away damp. Nothing was working out for her anymore. Valleyview had solved her family affairs, but not her own affairs. Her heart was in knots over Brett.

The phone rang. She crawled across the couch and picked up the receiver. Then she lay back on the pillows. "Yes."

"I've phoned you four times, I've left messages, don't you check your machine?"

"Brett." Kim sat up quickly. "Where are you calling from?"

"A hotel suite overlooking the lake. Are you free tonight?"

"Yes. I was going to play tennis, but no one . . . there's no one available to be my partner."

"Sorry. Tennis isn't one of my many talents." He chuckled.

"It's okay. I don't really need to play. Why are you in town?"

"On some important business."

"Well, it's nice to hear from you."

"We'll see one another of course. I thought you could give me a tour of your favorite galleries tomorrow. I know you have an appreciation for art."

Did she want to see him? Yes, she did, so much. She clutched her receiver to her ear. "That would be great, Brett. Shall I meet you somewhere?"

"I'll come to your apartment in the morning. We'll go out for breakfast."

"Okay."

"See you tomorrow then, honey."

Honey. As soon as she hung up the phone, Kim burst into tears.

The night seemed interminably long. But she was ready and waiting for Brett when he arrived quite early. She had put on a pair of cream slacks and bright green blouse. She had left her hair loose. She felt quite sprightly, but she thought he looked tired. Weariness slumped his broad shoulders beneath his shirt and light golf windbreaker as she offered him a cup of coffee.

"No. Let's go out," he said.

"This place is a bit rundown, I agree."

"It's fine, Kim. I just want to be with you. All right? And it's a great spring day."

She frowned at him. "What's happened?"

"Nothing's happened."

They took a cab to his hotel for breakfast. Kim rarely ate breakfast and enjoyed the big meal, sitting in armchairs at a small table overlooking the water. Brett had a lot to tell her about Josie and Brand. About how his parents were enjoying their cruise. How Princess missed Kim.

"Now, come on. I only rode her twice."

"She's playing up," Brett said, putting down his coffee cup in the saucer. "You should come home for a weekend and see her."

"I can't get any more vacation, especially now with this new position."

He leaned back casually in the armchair. "How is the new position coming along?"

"Oh, fine."

"That's good. You don't regret not taking my offer?"

Of course she did. "Did you fill the position?"

"No. Not yet. I haven't really worked on it much. Dad had a lot of things to go over with me before he left. Anyway, why don't we get going and explore the town?"

Kim had to admit by the time they ate a late lunch in an elite little restaurant, she'd had a great time. Brett was as interested in art galleries as she was herself. He even didn't mind a bit of shopping in some of the big department stores. He bought a little something for Brand and Josie.

"As if they haven't got anything," Kim joked.

"Poor things, hmmm? What do you want?"

He had his arm around her shoulder.

"What do you mean?"

"I want to buy you something."

"No, Brett. No. I don't need anything."

"How about an engagement ring?"

Kim did a double-take.

Brett smiled. "You know one of those circles with precious stones in them. Like your sister has."

Kim moved a few inches away from him. Saturday crowds pushed past them. Had they any idea what Brett Stanton had just said? "Why?" she asked.

"Because I want us to get married. You won't accept my job, so marry me instead."

"Then you could get me to work for Stanton Farm for free?"

"No. I wouldn't do that. I would use all my

love and persuasion as well as a good salary to entice you to take the job. I wouldn't expect you to marry me without a good job with good prospects and a good salary. I wouldn't ever want you to think you were beneath me in any way. We have to be equal."

"Brett. I can't marry you."

"One reason why not?"

Then Kim began to laugh. "I can't think of one."

"You mean the chip on your shoulder has been completely demolished?"

"Well and truly, Brett."

He moved closer to her and took her hand. "Let's go get the ring. I'm not leaving Chicago without being engaged to you."

"I haven't said I will, yet," Kim complained as he propelled her to the jewelry section.

"Say yes then."

"Yes then."

He bought her a single diamond that needed to be sized, but it was all paid for and Kim only had to return at the end of next week to pick it up. After that, they went back to her apartment.

"I wonder how many women have been proposed to in a crowded department store?" Kim said.

Brett put his arms around her and kissed her.

"I hope it's only you, but I couldn't wait any longer to finish my important business."

"I was your important business?"

"You better believe it you were. I've been in love with you for so long, Kim. When you used to come to the house with your mother, I was really intrigued with you."

She shook her head. "Oh no, you weren't. That look on your face when we left that evening proved that."

He frowned. "What look?"

"The look of disdain for me."

"Disdain? Oh, sweetheart, I never felt disdain. I felt sorrow and pain. That was me aching inside because I probably wouldn't see you again in the house. And I obviously couldn't go after you in that situation. I was off to college anyway. When Josie and Brand told me they were getting married, I thought I might have a chance with you again. I hoped."

"I think I always loved you as well, Brett. I think I was fighting attraction for a man I didn't think I could ever have."

"Oh, darling. You can have me. Any which way you want."

Kim gave him a look from beneath lowered lashes. "Do I light your fire?"

"You burn me baby."

She laughed and went into his arms. Slowly her arms slid around his neck.

"Kiss me like you really mean it," he whispered.

For the first time she did.